The Girl on the Boat

Danielle Lincoln Hanna

Hearth & Homicide Press, LLC

Cover photography by Matt Mason Photography
www.MattMasonPhotography.com
Cover design by MaryDes
MaryDes.eu

This is a work of fiction. Names, characters, businesses, places, events, and incidents are either the products of the author's imagination or used in a fictitious manner. Any resemblance to actual persons, living or dead, or actual events is purely coincidental.

Hardcover: ISBN 978-1-7376089-3-6
Paperback: ISBN 978-1-7330813-7-5
eBook: ISBN 978-1-7330813-8-2

Books by Danielle Lincoln Hanna

The Mailboat Suspense Series

The Girl on the Boat: A Prequel Novella

Mailboat I: The End of the Pier

Mailboat II: The Silver Helm

Mailboat III: The Captain's Tale

Mailboat IV: The Shift in the Wind

Mailboat V: The End of Summer

Mailboat VI: *coming soon*

DanielleLincolnHanna.com/ShopNow

MAILBOAT

MONDAY, JUNE 10, 2013

CHAPTER ONE
STEPH

N ot even a dog barked tonight. Not a single call for service. Not so much as a car found in a no-parking zone. Telecommunicator Steph Buchanan leaned on her hand at her desk in the Communications Center and sipped more coffee, staring at the two dots on her screen that represented the two officers patrolling Lake Geneva. They'd been driving circles since their shift began, looking for something to do. It had been an hour since anyone touched the radio.

A light flickered below her monitors and her eyes dropped to the bank of illuminated switches. Peeling labels designated *lobby door, hall door,* etc. They glowed a light yellow-green, signaling she could flip the switch and unlock a door.

One had turned red. *Garage.*

There were only two ways to open any of the doors in the station. Steph could trigger them from her workstation. Or an officer could cue the door with the key cards they carried in their pockets. Around here, the butt-swipe dance was well-known. Cops walked rear-end-first into doors so the sensors at hip-height could scan their cards.

There was just one problem. There were only two officers on duty tonight. And Steph knew from the map on her monitor they were nowhere near the station.

She frowned at the red switch as it flashed back to yellow-green. Maybe one of the detectives or the lieutenant had come in. But two in the morning? That was odd. She looked up at the feeds from the security cameras, turning her eye to the one posted in the garage. Black and white SUVs sat in silent rows, facing the center aisle for fast deployment. Patrol bikes, used in the crowded tourist district near the lakefront, lined one wall, parked next to a pair of motorcycles.

At the far end of the garage, a door swung shut. Steph was just in time to see a leg and foot vanish through it and noted another switch turn red on her dashboard.

There was nothing through that door but locker rooms, the gym, evidence intake, and storage rooms. They didn't have security cameras in those rooms. No one but officers ever went there.

Steph's radio mic sat in a little stand on her desk. She pushed the button. "Forty-four o-six and forty-four ten, report your status."

Static crackled. "Forty-four o-six. I saw a black cat just now," Officer Dan Norton drolled.

"Forty-four ten. I saw it fifteen minutes ago in front of the bakery," Officer Shelby Serrano replied. "It looked highly suspicious. At next sighting, we should pull it over for questioning."

"Copy that," said Norton.

Steph rolled her eyes. She didn't feel like cop humor right now. "I'm just checking your GPS is working. Neither of you returned to the station, right?"

"Negative," they each reported in turn.

"Okay. Somebody walked in. Probably just the lieutenant. I think he said he'd be in early—I just didn't think this early. I'm taking five to check it out."

"Need backup?" Serrano asked.

It reminded Steph of her college days, walking across campus after dark. *Give me a minute,* another female classmate from your dorm would say. *I'll walk with you.* But Serrano's offer of camaraderie existed on a different plane; no one wanted to mess with the sisterhood of bad-ass butt-kickers that were female cops.

"Negative," Steph said. "I'm sure it's fine." It was far-fetched to think anyone could have entered the station besides an officer.

"Copy," Serrano said. "Radio if you change your mind."

"Ten-four." Steph stood up from her station and grabbed a portable radio. She turned the volume low; she wasn't sure why. Out in the hall, she opted against the elevator and took the stairs. They were quieter. On the lower level, she used her own key card and quietly pushed open the door to the patrol car bay. Automatic lights flickered alive, cold and white. The patrol units stared at her through blind headlights, silent, and yet she almost expected them to breathe, sigh, berate her for interrupting their slumber. She tip-toed across the garage to the far door, hip-checked the key card sensor, and pushed the door open. The hall beyond was dimly lit by recessed lights. She waited for her eyes to adjust, then crept forward.

Half the doors in this hallway, even Steph couldn't open. Only the men, for instance, had the combination to the men's locker room door; only the chief, the lieutenant, and the detectives had keys to the evidence and records storage rooms. One set of doors, Steph didn't care for much, the ones labeled MAINTENANCE. Something about changing air pressure from the heating unit caused those doors to rattle exactly when you weren't expecting. The veterans loved telling the newbies the doors were haunted.

Steph crept past them—quiet tonight—and around a bunch of two-by-fours leaning against the wall, God only knew why they were there. Maybe someone had planned to build more shelving in the storage rooms once upon a time.

She checked the knob to the evidence storage room. Tightly locked, as it should be. She peered to the door at the end of the hall. The records room was lined with boxes of paper files, row upon row of them, relics from the days before the Lake Geneva Police Department had standardized electronic systems.

The door was cracked open. This one was secured with a good, old-fashioned metal key. Either the lieutenant had entered with his key or the lock had been forced. A light bobbed inside as if it came from a phone or a flashlight.

"Hello?" she called before thinking it through. The lieutenant would have turned on the overhead lights.

The flash vanished. The room at the end of the hall went pitch black.

Steph lifted her radio to her lips, hand trembling, and said something she'd never said before. "LGPD, requesting backup."

The radio crackled quietly and Shelby Serrano's voice came over the air. "Ten four. ETA, ten minutes."

Steph let her hand drop to her side and watched the door like a hawk. She was a dispatcher. A telephone cop. She'd walked people through countless emergencies, but she'd always had the safety of a phone line between her and whatever was happening. Sometimes her butt clenched at what she heard on the other end of the line, her jaw screwed tight at her inability to do more than advise and wait. But she didn't have half the equipment the patrol officers did. She didn't have a gun. She didn't have handcuffs. She didn't so much as have a flashlight. All she had—all she ever had—was her radio.

A rattling bang split the air as dramatically as a gunshot. Steph's heart leapt into her throat and she whirled. The haunted doors. They rattled aggressively, fighting against their own latch as if skeletal hands demanded release.

Something hard struck the back of her head. Stars burst before her eyes. Then there was blackness and a sense that the floor was coming up to meet her.

CHAPTER TWO

BAILEY

T he Mailboat towered over me, all two decks
painted navy and white. Lake water splashed
along the hull and churned against the pier posts. My
heart pounded. Jumping off and getting the mail in the
box was the easy part, everybody knew that. But getting
back on board? Good luck.

The boat never stopped.

If you didn't gather your courage in time, you
could end up standing on the pier like a piece of deck
furniture. You might find yourself stupidly watching
the windows flash by, filled with the faces of tourists
eager to see the show or the splashdown. There was
nothing to focus on. Where did you put your hands?
Where did you put your feet? Not to mention that
gaping maw that was three feet of roiling water between
the boat and the pier.

But once the mail was in the box, you just had to go for it.

I'd never done this before.

All these terrors flashed through my mind in the time it took a cricket to breathe. I inhaled deeply and clenched my fists. Bounced on my heels. I could do this. I could do this! I took a step back, winding up for the spring, then pounded across the decking and flung myself over the watery gap between the pier and the boat.

Time slowed. Sunlight glinted off hungry, chomping waves, waiting for me to miss, to slip, to plummet into the ravished belly of the lake.

My fingers found the handrail, cold metal pressing into the grooves of my palms. My sneakers hit the rub board and its gritty, slip-proof surface. My body crashed into a window with a rattle of its metal casing. I'd made it. I'd made it! I paused half a second to soak in the shock and the glory of it all. As the Mailboat rocked gently in the water, me sticking to its side, relief washed down my spine. Maybe I could do this after all. Maybe I could be a for-real Lake Geneva mail jumper. A smile as wide as the lake spread across my face.

"You're doing it wrong," said a voice behind me.

I started and turned, facing a pier which the boat had never left behind—never left behind because it wasn't going anywhere—wasn't going anywhere because this wasn't a tour. And I wasn't a mail jumper.

But Baron Hackett was, the boy who'd coolly informed me I was screwing up my own dearest dream. He stood there, tanned as a sailor, arms like masts, a glittering diamond in his ear and all. His neck was almost too thick for the knotted leather strap he wore around it, a creamy cowrie shell fastened to the center. He was everything a mail jumper should be: cool, calm, athletic.

And me? I was the concessions girl. Right now, I was supposed to be stocking the Mailboat's snack bar for a private charter. Instead, my handcart sat on the pier, the frost on the sides of a dozen ice cream cartons slowly melting and running down.

On the shore beyond the pier, the Riviera Ballroom sat like a squatty old fortress, its arched and pillared windows blinking sleepily at the unfolding drama, just one of a million it must have witnessed over the past eighty years. It had already seen all the action. This was where the jazz bands used to come up from Chicago and the flapper girls used to swing the night away. Tied up all around me were the other boats of the cruise line fleet, steam launches and stern-wheeled paddle boats old enough to remember the Charleston and the Cakewalk before that and even the Virginia Reel. I doubted any of them cared that I wanted to shrivel up inside a clam shell right now and sink to the bottom of the lake.

Baron combed spiky black bangs out of his eyes, deep and mysterious as underwater caverns but glinting with humor like treasure you didn't expect to find. Maybe he thought my efforts at mail jumping were laughable. "You trying out tomorrow?" he asked.

I slid off the rub board onto the pier and backed up against a pier post. "Tryouts?" I rubbed my arm nervously. "Um... maybe?" At the start of every summer, the kids who worked at the cruise line had a chance to compete for a place on the elite mail jumping team.

Baron motioned toward the boat. "You'll hurt yourself doing it like that."

I didn't get it. "Huh?"

God, this conversation was weird on so many levels—besides me being an idiot. Baron didn't talk to people. He was way too cool for that. He was the quarterback on our high school football team at just sixteen, a year older than me. He was in the National Honor Society. His family owned a mansion on the lake—one of the newer ones on the South Shore that probably had an AI for a butler. "Jeeves, turn on the lights." You know, like that. His sister had been a teen star in a hit TV series. I'm not even kidding. Her first month at school, she brought her own security guard, until her family figured out this was Wisconsin and the crowning of Miss Cheese Days at the nearby Green County Cheese Fest was still a big deal.

And did I mention Baron was a mail jumper? Around here, that was bigger than homecoming king.

"Never run straight at the boat," he explained. "You gotta run at an angle. Because of momentum, you know?" He hovered a palm mid-air and pushed it forward like a little ship through the waves. "The boat's moving this way, right?"

I nodded. "Okay."

The first two fingers of Baron's other hand became a tiny person, running toward the pretend boat. "If you run straight at the boat and grab on, you'll swing backwards like a door on a hinge and slam into the side." The finger person rotated and banged into his thumb. I remembered how I'd smashed into the windows, even with the boat sitting still. "You'll be black and blue all over. Right? So you have to get your momentum going *with* the boat." The finger person tried again, this time running parallel to the boat a few steps before jumping on. "Run at an angle, see?"

I nodded and rubbed my arm some more, trying to massage away my nerves. Now that he explained it, I felt like an idiot. Did good mail jumping candidates automatically know this stuff? Maybe I wasn't cut out to be a mail jumper.

And yet it was all I wanted in the world.

A hearty laugh rang out from the next pier over. Already dying of embarrassment, I was relieved for an excuse to turn my eyes away from Baron. On the other pier, talking with our boss, stood a man in a white shirt with gold and blue stripes on the shoulders. Tommy Thomlin. His uniform was navy-smart, the creases in his sleeves and shorts no doubt measured with a ruler. But just as predictably as his strict attention to detail was the smile on his face as he laughed at something our boss had said, or just as likely, something he had said himself.

He'd been captain of the Mailboat almost fifty years, as reliable as the mail itself. It blew my mind. I'd lived in foster care since I was five, and in my world, people dumped you for any reason. Maybe I colored on the wall; wouldn't eat my veggies; came down with the flu and threw up in the car. I wasn't their child. They weren't obligated to keep me. A simple phone call magically made me somebody else's problem. My own parents had opted to let me be somebody else's problem. And now my mom was dead and my dad just a nameless, faceless, non-figure in my life.

I wasn't sure why, but I lived for those few tours I got to ride the Mailboat with Captain Tommy, sitting behind the snack bar with my chin in my palm and listening to his steady voice like a calming rain. I'd never had a real dad or a grandpa or even an uncle—but if I had, I'd want him to be like Tommy. All last summer, I'd dreamed of the day I would finally be eligible to try out for mail jumping.

And now that day was almost here and I didn't know sticks.

"So, are you going to be here tomorrow morning?" Baron asked. His voice jerked me back to reality like a hand reaching into the lake, pulling me to the surface. I'd basically forgotten I was in the middle of a conversation with anyone.

I looked up at his brawny form, his bright yet strangely veiled eyes. Maybe I wasn't tough enough to be a mail jumper. Maybe you needed to be strong and smart and popular like Baron. Maybe you needed to *be somebody*—and all my life I'd been a nobody, invisible to everyone, and frankly, I liked it better that way.

But still, I'd spent a whole summer selling peanuts just so I could try out as a mail jumper. So... was I going to be here?

I scrunched my sleeve in my fist and bit my lip. "I guess?"

Baron laughed and shook his head, his eyes dipping down. I noticed he had long, dark lashes—but that kind of detail only mattered to fashion models and Olympians, the kind of girls who were actually eligible to talk to Baron Hackett. The kind of girls who mattered.

"Well, I think you should try out," he said, his lashes sweeping up again in the way girls-who-mattered would notice. "Any kid who practices dry runs on the dock clearly wants to be a mail jumper."

What a funny idea. I should be a mail jumper because I wanted to be? I was the bobber on somebody else's fishing line—pulled this way and that by fish and by angler. When had I ever been allowed to want anything? But maybe that was the difference between Baron and me. He was allowed to want things, and then he just went and did them. Maybe that was how he was always in the school newspaper while I vended snacks.

Baron lifted his backpack from the pier to his shoulder. "Well, hope to see you tomorrow."

He turned to go. As he did, something small and white fluttered down from an open pocket on his backpack. As it flipped and flopped, I caught glimpses of a magnetic strip on one side. The card sailed towards the cracks in the pier.

"Hey!" I shouted more to the card than to Baron. I pounced forward and clapped both hands over it. Relief washed over me as I felt the plastic pressed firmly between my palms and the wooden boards.

What a silly credit card, trying to get away like that. It would have spent the rest of its life at the bottom of the lake, and what good would that have done it? Peeling back my hands, I looked at the plastic escapee, expecting to see either the magnetic strip or the string of numbers.

Instead, I saw the emblem of a sailboat inside a circle—the same image on the city's flag. Printed around the circle were the words CITY OF LAKE GENEVA POLICE DEPARTMENT. I flipped it over and looked at the magnetic strip again. What was this thing? It looked like the key cards they give you in hotels...

Baron's lips were parted in a little *O* and his thin black eyebrows arched, the way you would look if you were both surprised and embarrassed, as if the injured baby bunny you were hiding in your backpack had hopped out in the middle of chemistry class. (Not that I speak from experience.)

"Oh wow," he said, "thanks for catching that." He thrust his hand out.

"What is it?" I asked, standing, staring at the card still in my hands. What did it mean, police department...?

"It's nothing," Baron said. He snapped it out of my fingers and shoved it into his back pocket. "Uh... my dad uses a meeting room at City Hall."

Oh, well that made sense, I guess. City Hall and the police station were in the same building. And Baron's dad was the kind of guy who knew every politician, every financial big-wig, all the important people. I could see him needing to meet with the local lawmakers often enough to have his own key card to City Hall.

But then why did Baron have the card? And why did it say "Police Department" and not "City Hall"?

"Gotta run," Baron said. "See you tomorrow." He waved and made long strides down the pier.

I watched him jog away, my head still swimming with questions. Then I stared at the boat. It had suddenly transformed into a bargeful of intimidation. What was I doing, hoping to be a mail jumper? What was I doing,

wanting anything at all? I didn't even notice Tommy walk
down the pier and stand next to me.

"I think it's soft enough to scoop now," he said.

I jerked my head around. "Huh?"

He grinned and nodded at my hand cart. The
cardboard ice cream tubs were going slouchy. I let out
a little wail and dashed to pull off a lid. The pecan
praline was swimming in pools of its own melted goo. My
heart sank. A good mail jumper needed to be sharp—and
I couldn't even keep ice cream frozen. Would this be
counted against me tomorrow?

Tommy chuckled. "If you hurry, I think it's
salvageable." He nodded to the aft deck of the Mailboat.
"Go put it in the freezer."

I crammed the lid back on and hurried to shove the
hand cart up the ramp. On board the small, enclosed rear
deck, I knelt on the floor behind the snack bar, flung open
the little freezer, and began unloading ice cream. From the
corner of my eye, I saw Tommy arranging tables and chairs
on the main deck, a short flight of stairs below me.

A ring tone jingled. Tommy took his cell phone out
of the holder on his belt, looked at the screen, and picked
up the call. "Well, good morning, sir," he said cheerfully.
"What can I do for you?"

There was silence as the other person talked. I knocked
a chunk of ice off the side of the freezer so I could fit one
more tub of ice cream.

"Last night?" Tommy said, as if repeating the caller's words. The tone of his voice had changed. All of a sudden, it was really heavy and serious, like a stone dropped into the lake. I peeked around the counter. Tommy had stopped arranging chairs and stood in the middle of the deck. He listened a while longer, a hand on his belt, then pulled a chair out from a table and sat down. "Is she okay?"

This sounded serious, whatever it was. Maybe a friend was sick? A family member?

Tommy shook his head at whatever his friend was saying. "No, I haven't heard the kids say anything. But I'll keep my ears open." He waved his fingers slightly, as if brushing a thought away. "Oh, don't mention it." As his friend continued to speak, Tommy's brow went heavy. His lips parted slightly, but his jaw went tight, as if he were ready to bite something off. I held my breath. It took something serious to get him mad, yet me and the other kids knew better than to cross him. He ran this boat like it was the Navy. "Wade, don't be ridiculous. None of these kids would break into a police station, much less attack a dispatcher."

Attack a dispatcher? Wow, that was pretty serious.
Wait...

Ice shot through my veins, and I was pretty sure it had nothing to do with the ice cream. I ducked back behind the snack bar and leaned against the shelves, my heart beating fast.

Baron...?

No, what was I thinking? This was Baron Hackett
we were talking about. He was the golden boy. The
top student in his class—in the entire school. The
future President of the United States, for gosh sake. He
wouldn't.

But he had a key card. And it said *Police Department*,
not *City Hall*...

Chapter Three
MONICA

"Have you ever seen the person in this photo?"

The homeowner sighed like he'd love nothing more than for me to clear off his porch so he could get to work. I drummed my fingers on the detective's badge clipped to my belt, equally impatient, and didn't so much as shuffle my feet apologetically. Well, screw him. It wasn't *his* co-worker who'd been smacked on the skull with a two-by-four and sent to the ER with a concussion. We were family at the PD, a tight-knit pack—though I was less the nurturing mother wolf and more the crazed hellhound bent on retribution. *Don't piss off Monica Steele* was practically the first thing they taught the rookies, and the last thing I'd ever taught my asshole of an ex.

The man set down his briefcase then snatched the photo out of my hand and screwed up his eyes. "You're kidding, right?" he said, snapping the print-out with his fingernail. "This is the back of his head."

Gee, really? I could also have pointed out that the individual from the security camera footage had pulled up the hood of their sweatshirt, obscuring even their hair cut and color, and had never turned their eyes up higher than the floor. I didn't so much as know whether it was a man or a woman. "It's the best we have," I said, my lips moving naturally—smiling, even—but my molars grinding together.

This was a joke and I knew it, knocking door-to-door with that stupid excuse of a mugshot. But this was me we were talking about. If I had so much as a scrap of a clue, I'd lock my jaws on it like a tenacious dog.

"Did you see anything suspicious last night?"

The man shook his head. "All quiet."

It was the same story on every street—the few streets we had the luxury of getting stories from. The Lake Geneva Police Station was located in the middle of a lot of businesses and parking lots. The building with the best view of our back door—the door that had been accessed by the perpetrator—was the Geneva Lake Museum, a long, low, red brick building across the street. But no one staffed that building until ten a.m., unless you counted the plush Dalmatian that sat on the front seat of a nineteen-teens fire engine.

With so few doors to turn to, my partner and I had broadened our search to include the nearest residential streets, a few blocks away. But so far from the station, I may as well show my crappy photo to the cracks in the sidewalk.

I tucked the picture back into my black leather portfolio, snapped it shut, and nodded at the homeowner. "Thanks for your time. If you think of anything, just give us a call." I handed him a business card. We said a brief good-bye and he grabbed up his briefcase before I was even off his porch.

I strode down the sidewalk back to the PD, cursing my luck. Our station was bristling with security cameras inside and out, yet all we had was the shadowy image of a tall, thin person in black sweat pants and a black hoodie. Steph had never seen him or her at all. The fact that someone had successfully snuck under our radar boiled my blood. And the big question: What had they wanted?

Back at the station, my partner, Detective Sergeant Stan Lehman, leaned against the pale brickwork near the employee entrance, enjoying the shade of a nearby tree.

"Great morning for a stroll, eh?" he said, twirling a pocket-sized spiral-bound notebook between his finger and thumb. After each spin, he tapped the notebook on his thigh, sliding his fingers to the opposite end. Started over. The pages of his notebook must be as empty as mine.

Like me, he wore tan dress pants and a black polo shirt, a badge embroidered on the left breast, his actual badge and service weapon carried on his belt. Unlike me, the beginning of a midlife midriff pulled at his belt and his hair grew in spiky silver blades. You'd never know we were close in age, forty-something. But the women of my family were blessed with dark locks for life—my grandma had died with a full head of mahogany hair at the age of ninety. I pulled mine into a ponytail every morning and ran five miles along the lake shore. Years of the routine had left me ready to run to ground any perp who dared take to his heels. Old Man Lehman was lucky to have me for a partner.

I cut to the chase. "Leads?"

"Nothing."

"Anybody report their key card missing?" Neither the door into the garage nor the one to the downstairs hallway had been forced; someone had used a key card. Which meant either one of our staff was missing one—or worse; one of our own officers had attacked Steph Buchanan.

Lehman looked past me to the parking lot and ran his tongue over his teeth thoughtfully. "I got a funny feeling someone's *about* to report a key card missing."

I turned. A tiny red Chevy two-door, the kind of just-functional junker you got saddled with in college, swerved into a stall and jerked to a halt. The door sprang open and Chad Rauch stepped out, a striking contrast to his ride. He wasn't on the schedule today, yet he was dressed head-to-toe in uniform, hat and all, every scrap of leather and metal polished to a high shine, black hair freshly buzzed. I was pretty sure military experience wasn't in his past, but, damn, it could have been. A smart young professional like that deserved a better set of wheels.

He walked straight up to us, shoulders square, hat tucked smartly under his arm. He looked Lehman straight in the eye—addressing him not because Lehman was male and technically outranked me, but because the new recruits were well aware my wrath was not to be tampered with. Despite turning to the more lenient of his superiors, his face was bloodless.

"Detective Sergeant Lehman, sir," he said.

Lehman worked his jaw and tapped his notebook against his thigh. "You lost a key card, didn't you?"

The boy's face melted like wax that had been warming in the sun, the gooey innards finally spilling through the fake outer shell. He suddenly looked like the twenty-one-year-old kid he was. On second thought, he totally deserved the junker. "Yes, sir," he said, and for a moment, I thought he might actually cry. He'd only been signed off by his Field Training Officer last week.

"How'd you lose it?" Lehman asked.

Rauch took a shaky breath and motioned with his hands as if wading through a marsh. "I-I don't know," he stammered. "I had it yesterday. Today it's gone."

Lehman sighed and nodded patiently. "Well, go check your locker before you run around confessing sins." He pushed off the wall, pulled open the door, and waved Rauch through.

The boy's face dawned with hope. "My locker. Yes, sir." He bounced on his heels then charged through the door.

"Five bucks says it isn't in his locker," Lehman commented when he was gone.

"I'll keep my five," I countered. I pushed my hands into my hips, stretching my back. "Well, wherever that missing key card is, we have a bigger question on our hands."

"What the perp wanted?"

I nodded. "He went straight to the records room. He wanted info on a case. An old case. But which one?"

Lehman's face crumpled into a pout that looked pathetic on a forty-year-old man. "I have a bad feeling I know where this is going."

I grinned and pulled a key from my pocket—a good, old-fashioned metal one—and held it up, its teeth catching sunlight. During our initial processing of the records storage room, nothing had looked obviously out of place. But maybe the perpetrator had left a folder sticking out. A page dog-eared. I shifted an inviting eyebrow at Lehman. "Ready to sift through fifty years of paper records with me?" The tenacious dog had latched onto its next victim.

Lehman ground his palms into his eyes. "Oh, God, shoot me now."

Chapter Four
TOMMY

S ettled into my captain's chair, I drummed my
fingers on the worn wood of the helm. Classic,
big-band jazz crooned over the sound system while
the passengers behind me chatted and laughed at their
linen-draped tables, spoons clinking on crystal bowls.
The broad windshield of the Mailboat gave me a
panoramic view of the lake; on a Monday morning,
the water was calm as a painting. The rambling old
mansions of the North Shore gazed silently, most of the
homeowners at work in Chicago for the week.

I sighed. It was too quiet around here. Our client,
hosting a business outing from Racine, had requested a
cruise with no tour. Otherwise, one of the kids would
be sitting on the tall stool next to me to read the
well-thumbed script. Those who had worked several

summers barely glanced at it anymore. I hadn't touched it in forty-odd years.

Tomorrow, a dozen kids would take their turns in the mail jumper's chair, some for the first time. Both pedestal and podium, it would be the focus of attention while the candidates were judged for their skills in presentation. But first, the white-painted piers would serve as stage for our cast of fleet-footed actors. I never knew who I'd end up working with, though jumpers from past years were generally a shoe-in. For the newbies, I'd give my two cents on who was ready for the job and who wasn't, but the decision was ultimately in the hands of the boss and a few honorary judges—people who had jumped mail while I was still in rompers, or so I doggedly maintained. These three or four individuals dictated who kept me company the rest of the summer and who went back to selling tickets.

By and large, I believed in letting the waves bring to shore whatever they may. The currents of life flowed too strong for those of us caught up in it to protest the details. Still, there was one kid I hoped would make the team this year...

I turned in my seat to sight down the aisle between the tables, up the short flight of stairs, and straight to the aft deck. I could just see the concessions counter. Bailey sat behind it, chin in her palm, strands of wavy brown hair escaping her pony tail as they usually did, the lake humidity playing its favorite game with her. She stared blankly at the countertop while twirling an ice cream scoop in a bowl.

The tables had all been served. The passengers were happy. And my mail jumper's chair was empty. No point Bailey sitting back there bored.

I picked up a microphone, lying within arm's reach on the counter beside the helm. My voice sounded over the jazz music. "Bailey, will you come fore, please?"

I waited for her to look up, but she continued twirling the ice cream scoop as if she hadn't heard me. I was about to page her again when she jolted in her seat, as if the speed of sound had slowed considerably from what I learned in school. Her eyes, round as a kitten's, flashed up and stared down the length of the boat. Finding me looking at her, she pointed to herself, raising her eyebrows.

I laughed. Typical of Bailey, so lost in her own world that there was a delay between her ears and her head. In confirmation to her pantomimed question, I jerked my head towards the bow.

She slid off her stool behind the snack bar, jogged down the stairs, and scurried up the aisle. "Yes?" she asked, eyes still wide. I swore, half the time she thought she was in trouble.

"Grab a seat," I said, slapping the backrest of the mail jumper's chair.

Obediently, she hopped onto the high stool, tucking her hands under her thighs. Her seat conveniently faced the deck where she could keep an eye on the passengers while I faced forward, reading the surface of the lake.

"Yes?" she said again, like the freshest of seaman recruits eager to be issued her orders.

Well, so long as she thought I'd brought her here for a purpose, I may as well play along. Nothing wrong with putting kids to honest work. "You practiced that script yet?" I nodded to the white ring binder on the counter, smudged black at the edges from countless fingers.

"Practiced?" she echoed. Her face hadn't lost the look of a tarsier, eyes impossibly round.

"You're trying out for mail jumper tomorrow, aren't you?"

She nodded. "Yes, sir."

"It's Tommy," I corrected, then bit my tongue before the mantra of every NCO in the Navy could spring to my lips: *Don't call me "sir"; I work for a living.* The title *sir* was reserved for commissioned officers—something I had never been. The captain's bars now perched on my shoulders were only an honorific, by my reckoning.

"Huh?" she asked.

"You can call me Tommy," I repeated. "It's what everybody calls me."

She nodded her head. "Yes, sir."

I looked out the side window and ran a hand over my mouth to smother laughter. At all times, Bailey marched a beat behind the band and I had to admit, it humored me. Yes, I'd be very disappointed if she didn't make the team.

I'd fought hard to learn how to laugh again. I forgot how after I lost my son and my wife within a few years of each other. But even now, laughter felt forced. A barricade. If you acted all right, people thought you were all right. They never probed into the disappointments, the hurt, the anger that lay just below the mirrored surface.

But something about Bailey's world was upside-down, inside-out. She constantly caught me off guard, surprised me. I laughed freely around her, the way I used to long ago.

"So," I tried again, "did you practice the script?"

"Oh!" she squeaked. "I didn't know I was supposed to." Twisting in her seat, she grabbed the binder off the counter, plopped it into her lap, and flipped to the beginning. As she crouched over the book, her eyes flashed back and forth over the text, lips muttering, as she read to herself and not to me.

She was taut as a hawser. In her eagerness to please, she'd probably send all her chances marching right off the end of the plank—a risk I couldn't let her take. "Sit up straight," I coached.

She sprang to attention without pausing for breath or taking her eyes from the book.

"Slow down. Breathe a little."

She closed her lips and breathed in deeply through her nose. Then she began to read out loud in a steady, clear voice. "'The Prairie-style building behind the park is the Lake Geneva Public Library, designed by James Dresser, a student of Frank Lloyd Wright.'"

I grinned, proud of how quickly she'd improved. "Good," I said. "Look at the passengers now and again."

She paused, mouth open, and flashed her eyes toward the tables. The chatter didn't abate, and without the use of the microphone it was safe to assume the men and women in business suits hadn't so much as noticed her. Still, as if intimidated by what she saw, she dropped her eyes immediately to the page. Her voice lost volume and wavered. "'The land and the original building were donated by—'"

"You're not worried, are you?" I asked.

Bailey's shoulders slouched as if she were visibly curling up inside herself. She nodded.

Something in my chest twinged for her. The way it had when my son had worried about making the high school football team. He'd turned out to be a darn good running back, despite my hopes he'd sign up for baseball. I never did understand the brutish sport of chasing the pigskin, but it had been a passion of his so I let him have his way in the end. I hadn't attended a lot of games, though.

I looked away and licked my lips. "You'll do fine," I said, remembering now that I'd never said those words to my son. His worries had been my worries—but he never knew it. I didn't let it show. I was a stubborn old curmudgeon back then. I still was. I watched the shore again, hoping Bailey wouldn't see me lost in memories—the kind submerged for years, covered in barnacles, razor-sharp.

She placed her finger in her page and closed the binder. "Tommy?" she asked. "How did they break in?"

I leaned closer, straining my ears. "What's that?" As usual, she was leaping from one bar of music to the next and I couldn't keep up.

"The police station," she said, her voice so low I could barely hear. She turned large brown eyes on me. "How'd they break in?"

For being so busy spinning her own tune, she apparently took in more of mine than I thought. She must have overheard my conversation this morning with Wade Erickson, the police chief and an old friend of mine. I'd promised to pass along any info the kids knew—but I had to admit, Bailey was the last person I'd thought would have any connection.

"I don't know how they broke in," I said. "I imagine that information's classified."

She narrowed her eyes suspiciously. "Classified?"

Well, that did make it sound like a spy thriller. "There's always something the police hold back from public knowledge," I said, a fact I'd learned from Wade.

"That way, they can confirm whether they've got the right person once they take in a suspect."

"Oh." She scrunched her nose in contemplation. "So… what happens when someone—you know, like a member of the public—thinks they know something?"

I slid my eyes her direction. Shoulders rounded, she frowned down at the binder. There was only one reason she'd ask such a question. "You should call the police station," I said pointedly.

She morphed back into the tarsier, as if the thought of calling the police frightened her more than addressing the passengers while reading the script.

I shifted in my seat to face her and studied the side of her face. Wisps of mousy brown hair framed her cheeks like a curtain. "Bailey, what do you know?"

"Nothing, really." I was about to mark it as a lie, but then she lifted her head and looked at me. There was no deceit. Just worry and confusion. "What if I'm wrong? What if I get someone in trouble?"

Well, that was a fair enough concern for a teenage girl. I thought back to my own teen years. No doubt calling the police would feel like tattling. Like watching a sibling get grounded because you said something. I wondered if she knew just how serious this thing was—that Steph Buchanan spent her morning in the hospital, but could just as easily have been killed. I sighed and cast my gaze over the rolling blue waves. "The police will want to know anyway. They can sort out whether the information is relevant or not."

She dropped her gaze into her lap and nodded.

I cast a glance her way. How could Bailey of all people have gotten dragged into this? "Who are you afraid of getting into trouble?" I asked.

She only bit her lips together and shook her head.

"You won't tell me?"

She studied the warped edges of the binder in silence. Shook her head again.

I sighed and grabbed a worn old envelope off the counter and wrote on it. "Here," I said. "That's the number to the police station." I'd known Chief Wade Erickson since he was a rookie—longer. As such, I'd memorized the number to the station long before there were smart phones. I inserted the paper between Bailey's thumb and the binder. "Call them." It wasn't a suggestion.

Bailey nodded.

I studied her downcast face. She was too young to worry about things like break-ins, assaults, police investigations. Her mind should be filled with the future, with possibility, with opportunity. What she wanted to study next fall. What she wanted to study in college. What career she wanted to go into. And yes, whether she'd make the mail jumping team tomorrow. But the question now stuck in her head seemed to weigh her down like an anchor on a line too short to reach the bottom. I couldn't stand to see her this way.

"Go on," I said, nodding at the binder. "'The land and the original building for the library were donated by...?'"

Bailey straightened her back and flipped open the book. She resumed her clear, steady voice. "'The land and the original building were donated by Mary Sturges, with the understanding that they would remain a public park and library forever...'"

I let the well-known words sink into my soul, shaded in the tones of a new young voice. I'd weathered storms, losses, nightmares. I'd learned to let the waves wash ashore whatever they may, to watch with disinterest, to pretend to laugh.

I couldn't pretend I didn't care whether Bailey made the team.

Chapter Five
MONICA

M y hands encased in nitrile gloves, I pulled out one cardboard box after another, peeled off the lids, and flipped through the contents. There was no way to tell whether a record was missing aside from checking each and every call-for-service number from each and every year, including our earliest documents—yellowing pages dated to the 1960s.

It was the kind of tedious work my undiagnosed OCD delighted in.

A few feet down the row, Lehman shoved a box back onto its shelf. "Did you know a cow got loose downtown in 1968?"

"That so?" I asked, my eyes and fingers scanning numbers.

"Yep. Farmer Willard Tillman's cow. Name of Annabelle, a doe-eyed Jersey who made the best cheese in four counties. They herded her onto the Riviera Pier where she jumped off and swam ashore, right into her daddy's waiting arms—well, his trailer, anyway."

"Good for her."

Lehman sighed and leaned against a shelf. "You're welcome, by the way."

"For what?"

"Helping you with this. Rock-turning is your department. I'm more of an interviews and interrogations guy; you know that."

"That's only because people couldn't hate your ass any more than they already do." Prying away at people's secrets didn't win you friends. "And I might point out, you have no one to interrogate until we pick up a lead."

"Touché."

I waved to the next shelf. "Nineteen sixty-nine is waiting."

He sighed and pulled out another box, cardboard sliding on particle board and metal. "You've seen the security footage. The perp couldn't have been in here more than five minutes before Steph showed up. He didn't have a chance to find whatever he was after."

"You don't know that."

He leaned his arm on the shelving. "Why do you always consider the impossible to be the likely?"

"You're the one who told me a cow dove off the Riviera Pier."

He hung his head and shook it side-to-side. "I wish I hadn't told you that."

Lehman was the big-picture guy. I was into the details. In theory, that should have made us a great team. Instead, we were trapped in a constant push-pull, one of us railroading the other into whatever we wanted. I usually won, but Lehman spent the rest of the time griping.

An hour later, our fingers flying through the nineties, Lehman was singing just loud enough for me to hear. "Oh, bury me not... Under lock and key... Where paperwork howls... And reports blow free..."

He'd been improvising lyrics for the past fifteen minutes and I was ready to cram a box over his head. A scathing comment about to fly off my tongue, I bit it short as my eye finally caught what I'd been looking for.

A loose sheet of paper, half out of its box, torn at the corner where a staple used to be.

I pulled the sheet free. The header on top listed the date as August 29th, 1995, the page number as three of three. The print-out began mid-sentence, the first sheet missing from the report.

...resisted arrest by refusing to follow orders and struggling as I attempted to put on the handcuffs. Officer Steele arrived at the scene at this time and assisted and we then were able to contain the subject. The subject was identified via his driver's license as Roger Ridley Holland. His rights were read to him at this time...

My eyes flashed to the signature at the bottom of the report. Sergeant Horace Stubbs.

"Oh, my God," I breathed.

The cop's version of the cowboy lament died mid-verse. "What?" Lehman asked.

"Oh, shit."

He shoved his box back onto the shelf and came to peer over my shoulder. "What? What is it?"

I passed him the torn report. He scanned the type-written text. "The Holland Murder," he said, all business now.

"Murder?" I repeated. "Really, Lehman?" I felt the heat rising beneath my collar.

Lehman tilted an eyebrow at me. "Yes, Monica. So said a jury of his peers in a court of law."

I jabbed a finger at the signature. "So said Sergeant Stubbs, you mean."

Lehman raised his hands, one of them holding the torn page. "Whoa, whoa, whoa, let's dial this down a notch."

"Dial it down a notch?" I spat out. "I nearly lost my job over Stubbs." I pointed out a line from the report. 'Officer Steele'—that's me. And look—remember this?"

I stormed around the corner to a set of shelves against the wall, old personnel files. I'd been a stark rookie in 1995, still in my first year of probation, barely sturdy enough to carry a ballistic vest and duty belt without crumpling under the weight. I was finally a full-time cop, and I'd staked my fledgling career to blow the whistle. In Stubbs' folder, I knew I'd find my own written complaint—the one the lieutenant had brushed over. The one that had earmarked me as an over-zealous greenhorn. In that complaint, I had accused Stubbs of knowingly disturbing the crime scene. Of fabricating evidence. Of framing Roger Holland for murder instead of the accidental death it was. Holland was a baker, for God's sake, not a murderer. The victim had been his best friend.

I pulled out a box marked with the letter *S* and pawed for Stubbs' file. A moment later, my hands froze.

"It's gone," I said, disbelief filling my voice. "Stubbs' personnel file. The whole thing. It's gone." I felt as robbed as I had the day my lieutenant told me, *Yes, I've seen your complaint and filed it appropriately.*

Lehman glanced at the torn report in his hand. "I guess we know what the perp was after, then. Info on the Holland case."

I looked at my partner over my shoulder. "Where's Roger Holland now?"

Lehman shrugged. "Still up at the state pen, I think. They gave him life. But he'd be an old man now. What about Stubbs? Where's he?"

"Door County," I replied. "Retired to some cabin on the peninsula."

"Should I be disturbed you know that?" Lehman asked, hoisting an eyebrow.

I glared daggers at him. "I never take my eyes off a dirty cop. Especially one that got away."

Lehman rolled his head dismissively. "Monica, you could never prove he did it—or even why he'd want to."

"Sergeant Stubbs liked making things easy," I shot back. "Too easy. Why let the jury hang on murder versus accidental death when it could just be a nice, clean murder? He sentenced Roger Holland himself the night he walked onto the scene."

Lehman raised his hands again. "Okay, okay, let's not drudge up all the bad feelings right now. The important thing is, we've got leads." He lifted the ripped sheet still in his gloved hand and waved at it. "Maybe we even have fingerprints. We know what our burglar came for. The only question now is why."

"Holland's raising a new appeal," I said.

Lehman raised his eyebrows. "He is?"

"I don't know. But he could be. And Stubbs wants the records conveniently erased. He wants no evidence that Holland could use against him." I jabbed a thumb at myself. "He wants *my* record of complaint to disappear."

"Or," Lehman countered, "Holland's raising a new appeal and needs this evidence."

I shook my head, frowning. "His lawyer would be nuts. He could simply file a request for the police report."

"The report, yes," Lehman agreed, "but the personnel file?"

"So he stole it? I don't buy that. Stubbs, on the other hand… I worked with him, remember? He was so rotten inside, he stank. Plants shriveled when he walked by."

Lehman sighed. "Much as I enjoy discussing semantics…" He took down the *S* box from the shelf, placed it in my gloved hands, and laid the torn report on the lid. "This isn't our baby anymore. It's all getting turned over to D.C.I. now."

The Wisconsin Department of Criminal Investigations. We weren't allowed to investigate one of our own cops, even if he was retired. Conflicts of interest were the reason why—like my keen desire to turn Stubbs' spine into a twisty-tie and shove his head up his own ass.

I blew a strand of hair out of my face. "They better do it right. I catch one whiff of any half-assed police work, and I'll have their badges."

Lehman rolled his eyes. "Monica, your half-ass is an ass and a half to anyone else."

I raised an eyebrow. "Watch it, buster, or I'll have *you* for sexual harassment."

"Sexual harassment. Right." He turned me around by the shoulders and dug his index fingers into my back, nudging me towards the door and the evidence collection room down the hall. "You go stow those in evidence. I'll call D.C.I."

TUESDAY, JUNE 11, 2013

CHAPTER SIX

BAILEY

I was gonna throw up. I couldn't do this. I wasn't cut out to be a mail jumper.

Pacing the quay behind the Riviera, I watched the kids gather on the pier a few paces away. There was the boss. The judges. The people from the TV stations and the newspapers—they never missed the annual appointment of the famous Lake Geneva mail jumpers. I swung my arms and clapped my palms together while sucking air through my lips. This was it. Go time. I needed to get out there and join the show. It was time to do this thing!

I couldn't. I planted my back against one of the brick pillars and buried my face in my hands.

It was lousy weather for your first try at mail jumping. Woolly gray clouds hung low in the sky, occasionally spitting a little mist. The boards beneath my feet were dappled with water, as would be every pier around the lake.

What if my shoes didn't stick? What if I fell and broke my nose? My arm? My neck?

What if I didn't make the team?

Out on the pier, a reporter pushed a microphone towards Tommy. I was just close enough to overhear. "Are you going to take it easy on the newbies today?" I recognized the reporter as Tim Fairchild from WISN12. Another man standing behind him balanced a camera on his shoulder.

"Nah," Tommy said. "The run will do them good." He chuckled.

I stared at Tommy and felt a big, hungry hole in the pit of my stomach. Like when you haven't had a bar of chocolate in forever 'cause your foster parents save them all for the two-year-old 'cause *he's so darn cute!* and for some reason you've developed a ravenous craving for chocolate. I just wanted something good to happen in my life for once, you know?

A voice spoke behind me. "You came."

I jumped and whirled. Baron Hackett smiled, his arm casually thrown up against a brick pillar, his other hand hooked through the strap of his backpack. Like all the kids, like me, he was wearing navy shorts and a white polo shirt bearing the logo of the cruise line company. The cowrie shell on his necklace peeked out from between his collars and the diamond stud glittered in his ear.

"Uh... yeah," I squeaked. "Yeah, I came." *Why did you have that key card to the police station?* I swallowed hard and hoped my skull wasn't see-through.

He smiled—the kind of grin that would convince millions of the TV-viewing public to buy whatever aftershave he was advertising. "You'll do fine," he said with raised eyebrows and a big nod.

Was it that obvious I was nervous? Was my face green? Oh, God, maybe my skull *was* see-through...

"Look, uh..." He shuffled his feet uncertainly. I'd never thought Baron could feel uncertain. What was wrong? He was all but guaranteed a spot on the team. "I don't actually know if I'll be around much this summer."

I frowned. "Then why are you trying out?"

He shrugged. "Wishful thinking, maybe?" He grinned at me, a lop-sided smile that was sad and heartbreakingly beautiful all at once. His secretive, magical eyes connected with mine. Delved into my very soul. Searched me. Searched *for* me.

My heart turned into a chunk of ice, sending frozen tendrils into every extremity of my body. What was he saying? Why was he looking at me like that? Did he... Oh, God, did he *like* me?

My brain screamed that I didn't have an acceptance letter from Harvard, a requirement for any girl before she could be noticed by Baron Hackett, much less liked by him. What was he thinking? Couldn't he see the school newspaper headlines? *Prince Falls for Pauper—Hackett, Johnson a Couple?!*

I shook my head and stepped back from him.

Baron's face fell. "What's the matter?"

I stared at him wide-eyed. This didn't feel right. Nobody liked me. Nobody even liked me enough to keep me. Invisibility was the only world I knew how to function in. But how did you tell the king of Badger High to stuff it?

Worse, how did you tell him you thought maybe he was the one who broke into the police station? But of course I'd never say that. I hadn't even built up the courage yet to call the number Tommy had given me.

"Uh..." My mouth felt like sand. I glanced toward the Mailboat. "They're starting," I said, relieved for an out. "We should go."

He followed my gaze. Saw the kids stepping away from the reporters and gathering around our boss. Baron looked into my eyes again. He must have felt the wall of ice there 'cause he backed off. "You're right," he replied, and it was probably the nicest thing anyone had ever said to me.

We fell into step side-by-side but with an awkward, wonderful space between us. Baron's stride was straight and strong like always, as if nothing had happened. I was pretty sure I wobbled down the pier like a top running out of spin.

I reached into my pocket and touched a wad of paper, folded up into a tiny square. The envelope Tommy had given me with the number to the police station. Why did I have to be the one sucked into this whirlpool? Why was I the one who had to make this decision?

Chapter Seven
MONICA

I plopped into a chair, the vinyl seat packed hard by countless butts, and tore the wrapper off my breakfast burrito. I bit into the soft outer shell. Eggs and sausage hit my tongue while the torn edge of the burrito steamed. My breakfast choice matched my mood. With the case out of my hands now, I burned inside. I wanted to see Horace Stubbs earn his dues and I wanted to see someone pay for assaulting Steph Buchanan.

"Any news from D.C.I.?" I asked my partner.

Lehman poked a fork into a giant blueberry muffin. "They arrested Stubbs last night."

I bolted upright in my chair. "What?" Now *that* was what I called police work. I was ready to get on the phone right then and commend the investigating detectives to their superiors.

"No," said Lehman, grinning behind another mound of muffin, "but I couldn't help getting a rise out of you."

I bared my teeth. "I'll murder you."

"Eh, I've been on your hit list for years." He sipped his Triple Chocolate Mocha. "Seriously, what did you expect? We only handed the case over yesterday."

"I know." Leaning on my elbows, I brooded over my burrito. "I just can't stand not knowing what's going on."

He shook his head, pulling a long, mournful face. "Patience was never one of your virtues."

I lifted an eyebrow at him, unmoved by his observation.

"How about fishing? You should try it." He set his fork down and swallowed. "Mm. I caught this walleye last night..." He tapped his forefingers on the table about three feet apart, a boyish grin lighting up his face.

"You know there's only one way I'd ever go fishing," I said, keeping my eyes bland. "Barrel, Glock." I made a hand motion as if firing a gun and mouthed a shooting noise.

Lehman stared in blank horror. He glanced away to release a small burp, and with it, no doubt, some of his shock at my idea of angling. "Wow, that's bloody."

I grabbed a fork and stabbed it into my burrito, filling it with holes, my appetite vanished. "What if D.C.I. doesn't find enough evidence?" I fretted.

Lehman was still staring vacantly. "All those fillets, just..." He turned up his palms. "Mangled."

I slapped my fork down on the table. "I'm serious, Lehman. What if Stubbs walks free all over again?" I dug my fingers into my hair, nails baring down on my scalp. "My God, I would die. And right now, he's the only lead we've got on Steph's attack."

Lehman sighed, as if mentally saying a few moving words to the slaughtered fish before laying them to rest. Only then did he poke his muffin again and shrug. "Someone will report something on the burglar."

I turned angry eyes on him. "No one's going to report anything. We don't even have a decent picture of the perp to share on social media."

Lehman grinned sarcastically. "Well, maybe we can round up a few suspects into a barrel and you can shoot them."

I frowned. "You're not going to let that one drop, are you?"

"Some images can never be erased." Lehman sipped more mocha. "Seriously, Monica, quit worrying about it. The break this investigation needs is right around the corner." He popped the last bite of muffin into his mouth and pointed at me with his fork. "Just you see."

CHAPTER EIGHT
BAILEY

*W*oo! Yeah!

Whoops, hollers, and applause erupted as Melissa Kraft landed gracefully on the rub board. She shook out her glorious locks, brown with blond highlights, and strolled the narrow catwalk back towards the bow without so much as holding the hand rail. Her shoes hadn't skidded once on the wet pier. She hadn't fumbled for a second with the mail or the mailbox. Was it really as easy as she made it look? Then again, she was a junior in college who'd been jumping mail for six years. There was a good chance she actually knew what she was doing.

The other candidates sat in a cluster of white plastic chairs in the middle of the deck, Baron among them. Sitting crooked, he used an armrest for a backrest and the backrest for an armrest. He looked all casual. Assured.

Confident. Like Melissa, it was inconceivable he wouldn't make the team. But he listened to the other kids cavort without joining the conversation. The veterans verbally jockeyed for the worst prank ever played on a jumper: mailboxes tied shut with rubber bands, obstacle courses built out of deck furniture, and piers covered in fresh, white paint—not really a prank, but not fun, either, if you slipped and ended up with a white bum for the rest of the day.

The first-timers listened wide-eyed. Maybe mail jumping was more hazardous than we thought.

Sitting at the rear of the group, my back against the side of the boat, I listened and pretended to text on my phone. Hopefully no one knew I had no one to text with. But none of them noticed me. Thank God. Between Baron and tryouts, my brain was silently trying to explode.

The TV reporter, the one who had talked to Tommy, scanned the group and noticed I wasn't busy yammering with the others. He slipped into a chair beside me. "Tim Fairchild, WISN12," he said, sticking out his hand. "What's your name?"

I eyed his hand suspiciously but wasn't quite rude enough to reject it. Still, I didn't put any heart into my grip—if you could call it that. "I'm Bailey," I said.

"Is this your first time?" he asked.

I glared at the mic in his other hand, wanting to say *no* just so he'd go away. But given a direct question, I was pathetic at giving cagey answers. "Y-y-yeah?" I dragged the word out like a question, and that was the best I could do.

His grin spread ear-to-ear, like he'd struck gold or something. "Is it okay if we get an interview?"

"Uh..." I lifted a shoulder in a shrug, waiting for my brain to drum up an excuse.

But the reporter mistook the shrug for an okay. "Great, thanks. Clint!"

The cameraman scurried over, popped out a tripod, and secured his electronic contraption to the top. "Rolling," he muttered, his face glued to an eyepiece.

The reporter pushed his mic next to my mouth. "What's your full name?"

"Um... Bailey Johnson."

"Will you spell it for the camera, please?"

I did.

"Bailey, this is your first time trying out. What are you feeling?"

I stared blankly at Tim Fairchild, wondering why the universe was such an asshole. Out of all the questions he could have asked, why the one I was in no mood to talk about? With *anyone?* Much less with half the population of *Wisconsin?*

Well, Mr. Fairchild, I kind of feel like tying dumbbells to my ankles and throwing myself into the deepest part of the lake. I'm sure that's a normal feeling for first-time mail jumpers, right?

Fortunately, none of that was what came out of my mouth.

"A little nervous," was what I said.

"What's your biggest fear?"

How about suffering through three more years of high school with the stigma of having ratted out the most popular boy at Badger High? I could already see it now: The hate notes slipped into my locker. The books being knocked out of my hands on my way to every class. The grassroots campaign to make every minute of my life as miserable as possible. The fact that *literally everybody* would know who I was. Would be staring at me, noticing me, and while they were at it, *hating* me. I would be as un-invisible as a pile of dog poo in the middle of a banquet table.

But no. Being noticed, known, and hated by my whole school wasn't even the thing I feared most right now. I glanced up the boat at Tommy, standing at the helm, his back to me. That's what I was afraid of. I was afraid of Tommy standing with his back to me for the rest of the summer. For the rest of my life. I was afraid of being completely, utterly alone. A piece of forgotten driftwood. The unwanted kid. Like I had been my whole life.

Tim Fairchild's question was still waiting for an answer.

"I mean, slipping and falling off a pier would be pretty bad," I lied.

"Oo, yeah, that would hurt," the reporter said.

Yeah. Sure. But not as bad as the stuff I was actually afraid of. Not as much as the life I'd already been living for fifteen years.

"How do you think you'll do today?" the reporter went on. "Are you going to make the team?" He cocked his head towards the starboard side of the boat, where another jumper was getting ready out on the catwalk, an envelope in his hand.

Quit making it sound like it's so much fun, I wanted to snap. *This is hard. I don't know what I'll do if I don't make the team.* But an answer like that wouldn't have made any sense.

I shrugged. "I guess we'll find out."

The reporter lowered the mic, giving me hope this interview of torture was over. "Well, good luck today, Bailey."

I forced a smile. "Thanks." Personally, I thought all my answers—the out-loud ones—were boring and dumb. Maybe I'd be lucky and they'd toss the entire interview on the cutting room floor instead of putting it on the evening news.

Tim Fairchild and his cameraman stood up. "Here," Tim said, "Why don't we get some shots of this...?" They walked away.

When I looked around, Baron Hackett was staring right at me. His face was blank. He'd probably just been watching the interview. But I felt as if I were made of glass and he could see every angle of my soul—including all the answers I'd kept to myself.

I jumped out of my chair and hurried toward the back, pretending I had to go to the bathroom. I tucked myself into the tiny closet, pulled the pocket door shut behind me, and latched the hook and eye lock. I closed the lid to the toilet and sat on it, burying my face in my hands. I let the tears fall. This was too hard. And I was so alone.

No, I wasn't. The engines of the Mailboat rumbled below my feet. I could feel them through the floorboards, a great purr like a lion wrapping me up in its velvety paws, nesting my head in its silky mane. *There, there, child. I'm here. I'm always here.*

When I was down to only sniffles, I pulled the square of paper out of my pocket. Unfolded it. Stared down at the phone number written in Tommy's blocky handwriting. It was so dumb, how badly I just wanted to be around him more. To always feel the way I did when he was near. Calm. Happy. Peaceful. Not terrified of literally everything. As courageous as a child wrapped safely in a lion's paws.

You should call the police station, he'd said. His tone had left no room for argument. This was what he expected of me. He would have told me it didn't matter what the other kids at school thought of me, turning in their favorite classmate. It didn't even matter if the teachers were mad, digging up the dirt on their star pupil. Tommy expected me to do the right thing, no matter how hard it was.

I pulled out my phone, woke it up, and checked my reception, which was always spotty on the lake. If I had two bars or less, I wouldn't do it.

There were three bars. Dumb phone.

I glared daggers at the treacherous little icon in the upper right corner. Then I locked my jaws and pulled up the call app. I typed in the number and hit *send* before I could stop myself.

The line picked up almost immediately. "Lake Geneva Police Department," a woman's voice said on the other end.

Butterflies raced in giddy circles round and round my stomach. "Um, hi. I wanted to call in... um... It's something to do with the break-in the other night. At the police station."

"You wanted to report information?" the woman asked. Without losing the professional overtone, she sounded the tiniest bit eager.

"Yeah."

"One moment. Let me put you through to the detective's bureau."

No, don't put me on hold, I wanted to say. *What if I hang up before you guys pick up again? Do you have any idea how hard it was to work up the nerve?*

But instead, I heard myself say, "Thanks."

The line clicked subtly, rang twice, then clicked again.

"Detective Steele."

It was another woman's voice. This one was brusque. Clipped. The voice of someone who'd worn the badge of authority long enough to have zero tolerance for bullshit. Someone who would tan Baron Hackett's hide, hang it out to dry, then go grab a sammy for lunch—no chips, but I'll take avocado.

"Uh, hi." I stared at the bathroom door, suddenly finding the flowy patters of the woodgrain fascinating. Behind me, tiny raindrops tapped on the window. The engines continued to hum, offering their unwavering support, as if Tommy himself were watching over my shoulder, encouraging me on. "I wanted to report something about the break-in at the police station."

"Who am I speaking to, please?"

I bit my lip. "Can I, like, report anonymously?"

"Absolutely," the woman said. "Your name will be withheld from public record. However, I need your name and contact information in case I need to follow up with you after this phone call."

"Oh." Her assurance that no one would know I was the one who'd tattled didn't help. I couldn't erase the images of the whole school staring me down in the hallways, glaring, turning the cold shoulder. I didn't think I could survive being hated by literally everyone.

I took a deep breath and did one of the few daring things I've ever done. I ignored the detective's instructions and skipped ahead to the important part.

"You need to talk to Baron Hackett," I said, my voice wavering. "He's a student at Badger High. Oh, and he works at the cruise line. He…" *He has a key card. He broke into the police station.* I couldn't bring myself to say any of that. "He knows stuff," I finally settled, my voice nearly breaking in two. "'Kay, that's it."

"Wait—"

But I'd already taken the phone away from my ear. I stared at the little red phone icon, telling myself not to do it. And then I did it. I punched the button and ended the call.

And then I just sat there shaking, my stomach doing back flips. Thank God the toilet was handy.

A rap sounded on the door.

My eyes shot to the latch. My brain conjured images of Baron pounding on the other side. *Bailey Johnson, I know what you've done!*

But the voice that called through the door wasn't Baron's.

"Yo, Bailey, you're up!"

It was Melissa Kraft.

"I'm coming!" I called back, my voice shaking, relief and fear hitting me at once. Thank God, Baron didn't know. But I was supposed to go out there now and not kill myself delivering mail. Maybe I should just fall in the lake and never come up.

Melissa's footsteps walked away.

I folded in half over my arms and let the shudders run up and down my body. What had I done? How was I supposed to get through what I had to do next?

CHAPTER NINE
MONICA

S hit!

I called into the handset—"Hello? Hello?"—but the girl was gone. So I hung up and dialed the Communications Center. While it rang, I rapped a pen and stared at the wall of my cubicle. Nothing but a fuzzy gray backdrop, it was utterly devoid of photos, sticky notes, or (God forbid) succulents in tiny hanging vases. A clean space fostered a clear mind.

"Angie," I said when the telecommunicator picked up, "what's the phone number on that call you sent up to me?"

"Just a sec." Angie was silent while her computer mouse clicked in the background. "Oh... Oops."

Oops? What did *oops* mean? "What?"

"Um... I must have picked up too fast. The number didn't have a chance to register."

I braced my elbow on my desk and pinched the bridge of my nose. Angie had been working here for nine years. What was she doing making rookie mistakes?

"Sorry, Steele," she said, and I could hear her bracing for a tongue lashing.

"It's okay," I sighed. It wasn't. But I didn't have time for tirades. "Thanks for checking."

"Of course."

I hung up. "Shit!"

Lehman rolled away from his desk and peered around the divider between our cubicles. His, I knew, was littered with pics of his kids at various ages—his ex conveniently excluded—and magazine clippings of sports cars he'd never be able to afford. "What's wrong?" he asked.

"We've got a lead." I flipped open my portfolio and scribbled notes from the all-too-brief conversation.

Lehman spread his arms. "What'd I tell you! Someone had to know something."

"Yeah, but I don't have the PR's contact info."

"Oh. Well, shit," Lehman agreed.

I ripped the sheet from my notebook and handed it to him. "Call D.C.I. and pass that on to them." I turned to my computer and pulled up our driver's license database, clacking my keyboard furiously.

Lehman stuck on a pair of reading glasses and stared at my note. "So, our anonymous PR could provide evidence that this—" he frowned at my note "—Baron Hackett was the one who broke in?"

"No. She didn't even accuse him of anything. She just said, 'He knows stuff.'" I lifted my hands from my keyboard long enough to make air quotes. "But she was hella nervous. I think she was afraid of saying too much."

"Hmm. Well, I'll pass it on." He pushed off and rolled back to his own desk. His phone clicked out of its cradle.

"Wait," I said.

"What?"

I was staring at the info I needed. A search for Baron's driver's license had brought up his home address. From there, I'd hopped over to the county's database of properties and found the owner.

"Tell D.C.I. they might want to be careful," I said. "Looks like his dad's Richard Hackett."

"Who?" Lehman demanded from the other side of the divider. Most of our conversations took place with a wall between us, and I liked it better that way.

"Richard Hackett," I said. "He moved his family here about a year ago." I studied the map provided by the county property database. "Apparently they have one of the big houses on the South Shore. Hackett originally made his fortune in Silicon Valley. Then his daughter had a career in Hollywood. That's why they moved here, to get away from the hype. Now Hackett's an angel investor."

"Geez, what do you do, read the social column?"

"No, politics. Hackett's running for the county board of supervisors."

"Shit, do we have an election this fall?"

I rolled my eyes, leaned against the back of my chair, and spoke to the ceiling. "The point is, with Hackett's background, he's used to playing in the Big Leagues. The moment D.C.I. so much as asks to speak to Baron, his dad'll have the top lawyer in the country at his side in ten seconds."

Of course, Baron had the right to get a lawyer whenever he so chose. But whether Baron was innocent or guilty, it was a lot harder getting answers out of a lawyer than out of the lawyer's client.

"Oh. That's a good point. I'll give them the head's up."

"Thank you," I hissed under my breath and returned to my computer. With Lehman, there was no such thing as a simple conversation.

While he put in the call, I returned to my databases. My next stop was NCIC, or the National Crime Information Center, a phenomenal black hole of criminal information maintained by the FBI. I plugged Baron's name, driver's license, and license plate into every search I could think of: Criminal history, negative. Past arrests, negative. Warrants, negative. I finally tried a QQ—also known as a Query Query and the ultimate proof that cop speak is redundant. With the QQ, I could see the last se search *someone else* had made on Baron and where that cop or investigator was from. Maybe Baron had been pulled over for a traffic violation and some beat cop had run his license plate.

But even the QQ turned up a negative.

"Damn it," I muttered. Had he never so much as run out a parking meter?

I didn't notice Lehman hovering behind my chair until he slurped noisily out of the giant coffee mug he carried around the office. *Top Cop,* it said. I took umbrage with that mug.

"You realize D.C.I. will take care of all that?" he said, waving the mug at my screen.

"I'm curious, that's all."

"Well, just don't let curiosity kill the cop. There's a reason we handed this case over."

"If I find anything interesting, I'll turn it over to D.C.I."

Lehman shrugged. "Okay, I guess you're a big girl now. Oh, that reminds me, I got you a present." He snagged a rectangular box off the corner of his desk and plopped it onto the corner of mine. No bigger than his hand, it was wrapped in paper featuring a dozen varieties of fish.

I glanced between it and him. "What is this?"

"Open it."

I did. Inside the box was a foam fish, colored like a rainbow trout. Printed along the side were the words *Gone Fishin'.*

"It's a stress ball," Lehman explained. "Only it's a fish."

Eyes glazed, I stared at him. "Seriously?"

"Now you don't need your Glock."

I balled up the fish and threw it at the middle of his chest. Snickering, he beat a hasty retreat to his own desk. I left the fish abandoned in the middle of the floor and focused my attention once again on my screen. Out for blood now for any scrap of info I could find on Baron Hackett, I turned to Facebook and Twitter, then remembered to check this thing that was getting popular with teens, Instagram.

Baron's Facebook profile was shut up tight. I couldn't see anything beyond his profile picture and header image without friending him. Made sense. It sounded like the Hackett family had had problems with both the paparazzi and rabid fans in Hollywood. Baron apparently took his and his sister's security seriously.

His Twitter feed was almost as sparse. Maybe twice a month, he retweeted people like Elon Musk, Warren Buffet, and Tony Robbins. On occasion, he linked to various newspaper articles. On closer inspection, they were all about his family members. His dad's bid for office in Walworth County. His sister winning an acting award.

His father backing a zero-waste factory in Iowa. One article from the local paper showed how Baron himself was spearheading an effort by local teens to keep blue-green algae blooms from appearing on Geneva Lake. Another article from his days in California showed him as the spokesperson for a teen mission to help homeless youth in LA.

I clicked through to the website of the Lake Geneva Regional News and placed a search for Baron's name. During a ceremony at the high school last spring, Baron had won no fewer than three awards.

I frowned at my screen. This couldn't be the same kid who'd broken into our police station.

"Hello, hello, hello!" A cheerful voice broke the silence as a uniformed officer walked into the detective bureau, a cardboard box under his arm. Thirty-something, hair cropped military-style, he had the easy-going manner of a man whose job it was to be cool in the eyes of fifteen hundred teenagers. For nine months out of the year, Mark Neumiller was our school resource officer at Badger High, where he had an office. In the summer, when Lake Geneva could swell to three times its normal size, Neumiller served as a third detective in our bureau.

Lehman's chair groaned as he leaned back. "My God, they let you out of school? You passed your final exams?"

Neumiller grinned and pinched his fingers together. "Scraped by, just barely." He set the box on a third desk against the wall, shoving aside stacks of paper and a model of a red-hot Porsche. "Dude, seriously what is all this?"

Lehman waved casually at the clutter. "I'm utilizing departmental resources. You're not even at that desk for nine months out of the year."

"Okay, okay, I get it. But this spot is mine now, so shove this shit somewhere else."

Lehman groaned and got out of his chair, then began to stack the paperwork on his own desk.

Neumiller nodded across the room as he unpacked his cardboard box. "Steele, how's it going?"

I leaned around my cubicle wall, eyes narrowed. "Do you know Baron Hackett?"

Neumiller placed a family photo next to his computer monitor. "Baron? Sure. Everybody knows him. Why?"

"We just got an anonymous tip that he might be involved in our break-in."

Neumiller pulled a skeptical frown. "Probably some jealous classmate trying to take him down a peg. Baron's a straight-A student. Team quarterback. National Honor Society. He was school treasurer this year. Next year, he's running for president." Neumiller shrugged. "He's a good kid, you know? Everybody loves him."

I frowned and chewed a hangnail. This wasn't adding up. The girl I'd just talked to over the phone was almost too nervous to talk. Then again, she would be, if she was turning in the most popular boy in school. If personal experience had taught me anything, it was that people could change radically, even when you thought you knew them as well as your own soul. It was hard to believe sometimes that the man I'd married was the same asshole I'd eventually divorced.

Still, I was faced with two versions of Baron Hackett. Was one real, the other fake? If so... which one?

Chapter Ten
BAILEY

I slipped out of the bathroom and ran back up the main deck.

"There she is!" yelled Noah, a boy in my grade with blond hair and a smile that was way too confident and friendly for my comfort level. This was his first time trying out, too. "Bai-*ley*! Bai-*ley*!" He chanted and clapped his hands. The other kids joined in.

Oh, God, I was gonna die. I ducked my head and hurried past them, but couldn't take my eyes off Baron. He was still sideways in his chair, for all the world as if nothing earth-shattering had just happened. Nothing that would maybe alter the course of his life forever. He just gave me a grin and a nod, as if saying *You got this.*

My face felt numb and cold. I had to focus. *I never called the police station,* I told myself, as if it were true. *This is the day you've been waiting for—mail jumping. This is a really, really good day.* I tore my eyes from Baron and scuttled to the front of the boat. Tommy stood at the helm, guiding us in a lazy circle so I could run at the same pier everyone else had.

He cocked half a grin. "You ready?"

I bobbed my head—again, as if it were true. But I couldn't feel my extremities. Probably a bad thing for mail jumping.

Melissa held up my mock delivery, a bunch of envelopes rolled up inside a newspaper. A rubber band held the entire bundle together. She placed it firmly in my upturned hand. Thus bestowed with the scepter of the office I hoped to occupy, I scooted to the large square window at Tommy's right. As high as my hip, it sat wide open, the glass insert stowed against the wall on the opposite side of the boat.

I threw one leg over the sill. My outside foot found the rub board. My inside foot found the bracket bolted to the floor, like an upside-down stirrup. It had been specially mounted to help the mail jumpers keep steady. The wind whipped my hair and spit a fine mist into my face, some from the sky, some from the waves breaking under the bow. Under the rub board, the water rolled dark blue and foamy white. The shoreline and the piers whipped by.

Oh my God, I was sitting in the mail jumper's window. I hadn't expected it to feel so... exhilarating. Like a mermaid riding a charging seahorse. The Mailboat's engines rumbled through my bones. A grin spread across my lips as my whole body unexpectedly relaxed. This felt sooo good. So right. Like I'd been born for this. Like the Mailboat was part of me. Like the spirit of its wooden body ran through my veins.

Tommy pushed the two levers beside his helm. If he was slowing the boat down, I couldn't tell. The pier felt like it was speeding toward us. "Use as much runway as you need," Tommy said.

Instead of sticking straight out into the lake, this pier ran parallel to the shore, creating a slip for the owner's boat. In the middle of this runway was the mailbox. Fixed to the top of a pier post, it stared me down. I mean, literally. The box was shaped like a badger, a wooden craft-fair find painted black, white, and gray. Its little black feet hugged the mailbox and a dark shiny eye locked gazes with me.

Gripping the handrail above my head, I pulled my other leg through the window. I was standing on the rub board now, the lake flying beneath my feet. I held the mail in an iron grasp so there was no chance of it getting away.

Back in the boat, the kids clapped and cheered. "Go, Bailey! You can do it!"

"Just keep your eye on the pier," Tommy coached as it charged closer, a javelin waiting to unseat me.

"And don't forget to kiss the badger!" Melissa called.

Kiss the badger? Oh, yeah. It was a tradition. All the mail jumpers kissed the badger...

The first pier post swung by.

"There you go, right there." Was it just me, or was Tommy's voice tense? Why would *he* be nervous?

There was no time to think about it. I launched myself off the side of the boat. My feet hit the pier, but my body kept running as if the Mailboat had flung me away, a dog shaking water out of its fur. Momentum. Account for momentum! Isn't that what Baron had told me?

I'd run clear past the badger before I knew it, but it was okay. It was a long pier. I'd just reel myself in before I sailed clean off the end.

That's when my shoe slipped out from under me, the rainwater offering zero traction. My right hip crashed to the deck. Then just like a Slip n' Slide, I careened across the pier... over the white-painted boards... off the edge.

My yelp was choked off by lake water and cascades of bubbles.

Chapter Eleven
TOMMY

"O h-h-h-h-h!" the kids chorused and rushed to the windows.

Melissa sighed, shaking her head. "She didn't kiss the badger."

I didn't answer. My breath was caught in my throat. I kept one eye on the path of the boat, another on the place where Bailey had gone in. I didn't breathe again until Bailey surfaced. She came up like a fish catching flies, opening her mouth wide for air. A cheer rose from the other candidates as she doggy-paddled the few strokes to the ladder on the side of the pier.

She looked okay, thank goodness. That was a hard fall. I had no doubt she'd bear the battle wounds for a while. But the longer-lasting damage might be to her score. I glanced at the judges. They whispered to one another, shaking their heads, clicking their tongues, marking their clip boards.

I sighed. It was mail jumper tryouts. You were practically guaranteed a few kids would end up in the lake.

I'd just hoped it wouldn't be Bailey.

CHAPTER TWELVE
BAILEY

I n the end, I guess one splash into the lake wasn't the worst thing ever. Anyway, Celeste Jones fell in twice and forgot to grab outgoing mail once, so I had to be light years ahead of her.

She and I huddled on the Riviera Pier in a pair of beach towels one of the judges had been generous enough to bring along. The judges were still on the boat, their chairs huddled close on the main deck as they compared notes. Within moments, we would all know our fates.

"Well, I know *I'm* stocking potato chips this summer," Celeste said, teeth chattering. While we'd dried off some, it was still overcast and we hadn't warmed up at all. The drizzle clung to Celeste's tight, curly black hair like pearls and dripped gently on her terry cape.

I shrugged. "But your reading was really good." And it was. Standing instead of sitting, she had barely glanced at the script, even though she was new to it, and projected so clearly she wouldn't have needed the microphone. She even smiled at the audience—the judges, jumpers, and reporters. She seemed to know all the right places to pause, to talk a little softer, to talk a little louder. It was like a night at the theater, and I knew my own reading had been mud by comparison.

"Yeah, maybe I should stick to speech club," she said. "'Cause dang, I ain't no mermaid out on those piers!" She laughed, even slapped her knee. Her teeth flashed white against her warm brown skin.

I wished I could be as nonchalant. I had peeked once during my reading, and there had been nothing but eyes, real and electronic, all staring at me. My heart had pounded out of my chest. *Why are you all staring at me? What have I done wrong?* I wanted to ask. *Is it because I fell in? Because I reported Baron?* And my brain nearly tailspinned into a panic attack.

And then I'd caught a glimpse of Tommy out of the corner of my eye. He was steering us back to home port, staring over the lake, mouthing the script along with me, the way a parent does when their six-year-old is in the school Christmas pageant.

It was super tacky, and yet it worked. I remembered to sit up straight. To breathe slowly. I tried looking at the audience again, and it wasn't so scary. They looked like they were actually listening or something—which was the weirdest experience of my life. Maybe I was doing okay? Anyway, the next time I glanced at Tommy, the corner of his mouth was lifted in a tiny smile. The judges seemed to grin as well as they marked up their clip boards. Maybe there was hope?

Baron's reading had been last. He wasn't as flamboyant as Celeste, but he spoke in an even tone and didn't pick up the book at all. He had it memorized. As such, he was able to join eyes with the audience the entire time. He wasn't being a show-off, either. It was like he was just having a conversation. I was so scared he might look at *me* that I stared at my hands the whole time, crunched tight inside my fuzzy towel.

A stirring on the pier jolted me out of my mental performance review. Everyone was staring at the windows along the boat. Inside, the judges nodded all around, smiling at each other, and tucked their clip boards under their arms. They rose from their chairs. My heart hammered in my chest. Did I talk too fast during my reading? Did I skip lines? Did I forget to put the flag down on a mailbox? Did I fall off more piers than I remembered? It wouldn't be the first time I'd blanked out bad memories.

The judges filed down the gangplank. The cameras started rolling again. Our boss, Robb Landis, stood in the middle of the pier and rubbed his hands together. He wore a fairly normal-looking black rain jacket, but also a pair of salmon pink chino shorts and hemp-braided flip-flops.

His lakeside fashion was perfectly on point at all times and at the same time vaguely eccentric. "All right! Ladies and gentlemen, we have our results. First of all, thank you, candidates, for trying out today. You all put in your best, and it showed. It was a hard decision in the end."

But was it? Some of us had clearly done worse than others. I glanced between Celeste's terry towel and my own, then, as if seeking some kind of reassurance, I looked to Captain Tommy. Standing at the bow, he calmly uncoiled a huge electrical cable and plugged it into the port on the boat to recharge its massive batteries. Then he brushed his palms together and turned to watch. Like me, like all of us, he kept his eyes on Robb Landis.

"Okay," Robb said. "First up..." He glanced at the list one of the judges held and drummed his hands on a pier post, letting the sound rise to a crescendo. "Baron Hackett!"

In a show of solidarity, the kids burst into applause. The people working the cameras zoomed in for a shot of Baron's grinning face.

"Step on up here, Baron!" Robb motioned to the rub board on the side of the Mailboat. Baron quietly stepped into his assigned position, clasped one wrist in the opposite hand, and allowed another smile for the cameras. I imagined grace like that had been carefully cultivated in the environment of Baron's high-flying family. I knew if my name was called, I'd be smiling like an idiot.

"Our next mail jumper is... Melissa Kraft!"

Melissa smoothed a strand of brown-blond hair out of her face and stood on the rub board next to Baron.

"Mail jumper number three... Noah Cadigan!"

"Woo!" Noah pumped a fist and ran toward the Mailboat. Half-way across the pier, he did a cartwheel. Everybody laughed, and Noah hopped onto the rub board, smiling from ear-to-ear. Yep. That would be like me. Only if I tried a cartwheel I'd end up in the lake again.

Three spots filled. Only three to go. I bit my lips together.

Robb called out two more names. "Lacie Mulhullan!... Myles Trainer!"

One more slot. I closed my eyes. Please, God. I'd never ask for anything ever again. Just let me be a mail jumper...

"Okay," Rob said, "one more mail jumper will make the 2013 team. I just want to say again what a great job you all did. We're so proud of you and so happy you wanted to be on the team. Those of you not making it this year, we really do hope you'll try again next year. Okay, with that said, here's our final mail jumper."

My eyes were still closed. My jaw locked together. *Just this once, let something good happen.*

"Alisha McCormick!"

Alisha screamed and jogged to the Mailboat, joining the rest of the team on the rub board.

My heart broke cleanly in two, as if water had been pooling and freezing, forming a crack there all along. I hadn't made it.

I hadn't made it.

Robb spread out an arm toward the six kids standing on the side of the Mailboat. "Judges, ladies and gentlemen of the press, may I present the 2013 Lake Geneva mail jumpers!"

Cameras flashed and guys with recorders over their shoulders panned down the line of victors.

"Tommy, get over here." Robb waved. "They need a shot of the captain with his crew."

Tommy shook his head as if all the hoopla were a little ridiculous, but he obliged, stepping slowly up onto the rub board at the head of the line. More flashes. More minutes of footage. More smiling faces.

I would have given everything I owned to be standing where Baron stood, right beside the captain. Why did everybody else get wonderful things in life? Why did I always end up with the short straw? I fought back tears. I didn't want the camera crews or my boss to think I was a spoiled brat and having a fit.

I just...

I didn't want to be a foster kid anymore.

I didn't want to be alone anymore.

"You know, I'm kinda glad I didn't get the job," Celeste whispered in my ear. "I figured out last-minute I ain't got the nerve."

I tuned her out. I didn't have the nerve, either, and yet I was willing to find it, if only I could be a mail jumper.

But I wasn't.

Chapter Thirteen
TOMMY

A smile pasted onto my face for the benefit of the weekly paper, I tried to see past the flashing cameras. Tried to see Bailey. How was she taking it?

I finally spotted her beyond the throng of reporters. A striped blue and white towel clasped around her shoulders, she stared blankly at the new team. The single tear that slipped down her cheek told me all I needed to know. She'd worked hard for this. And her spot had been given to somebody else.

I wanted to tell her that it was okay. That she'd done well. That she could try again next year. But a year in the life of a teenager was, of course, forever. So I tried to think what else I could say. My mind drew a blank—other than to demand of myself why I cared at all.

I'd seen countless candidates turned away. Some eventually made the team. Others never tried again. The waves washed ashore whatever they may. It wasn't my place to care.

And yet I did. Maybe I was just a selfish old man, wanting to keep close to me the one person who could tempt a little joy from my dry and weathered soul, like sap running anew in long-dead driftwood. Maybe even I still wanted to dream now and again.

Chapter Fourteen
BARON

B aron rolled down the winding, oak-lined drive to
the house on the South Shore. A boxy, modernist
mansion painted dark taupe, the architect had broken up
its patterned lines by off-setting the picture windows.
From the inside, the vast sheets of glass practically brought
the lake and the woods indoors, mixing nature with
minimalism. It wasn't a bad place to call home.

Tonight, two extra cars sat in front of the garage.
Apparently the Hacketts had company. Not unusual. On
any given day of the week, Baron's mom might have
friends over or his dad might have brought home a
business associate.

Baron pulled up beside the extra cars and killed the
engine. Then he sat staring at the blue and white BMW
emblem in the middle of the steering wheel.

Today was hard.

After tryouts, he'd worked a full-lake tour on one of the paddle wheel boats. The slow sojourn around the lake had mostly provided a chance to dwell on the last few days. The stress simmering just below the surface. The exhaustion it brought on. But it wasn't in a Hackett's nature to be tired. *Work twice as hard as the competition.* That's what his parents had taught both him and his sister. It was their ethic. It's what had won Baron a spot on the mail jumping team and everything else he'd accomplished in life.

But he was sorry Bailey hadn't made the team, too. She had been nervous and it had interfered with her performance. But a single fall into the lake wasn't grounds for disqualification. Other candidates had simply been better.

Well, in good news, she might still have a chance. Depending on what fate had in store for Baron. Each second of the clock felt like a bomb ticking down toward an inevitable detonation. The only question was how many seconds were left. A million? A thousand? Ten? It depended whether Bailey had ever reported him. Some of the kids at school thought she was stupid because she was quiet. But they were wrong. She was an observer. She took in everything around her. The question was whether she ever let the things she knew back into the world again.

He grabbed his backpack, got out of the car, and mounted the beige-painted porch to the front door. As he walked into the living room with its vaulted ceiling and dark hardwood floors, the smell of steaks and sizzling onions greeted him, and with it laughter and conversation. Baron kicked off his shoes and walked around the massive, double-sided fireplace into the kitchen.

"There's our Baron!" exclaimed his mother's cousin, holding her arms out wide.

"Hey, Deb," Baron said, stepping into the hug. When she released him, her husband Jerry gave him a friendly slap on the shoulder. Baron exchanged nods with their son Chad, who sat at the black marble island with a beer. Baron's sister Regina sat next to him, dunking crackers in jalapeno dip.

"How were tryouts?" Baron's mom asked. Tonya Hackett stood behind the stove in the middle of the island, a petite woman with messy brown hair stuck through with chopsticks. Silver bangles glinted on her wrists and around her neck.

Baron joined her behind the stove and leaned in to give her a kiss. "Great. Made the team again."

The family erupted into cheers. While the Hacketts held high standards, they also offered high praise. It wasn't a bad arrangement.

"Nice job, Baron." His mom's smug smile said she'd known all along he wouldn't fail.

"Will we see you on the news tonight?" Baron's father, Richard Hackett, was still wearing his business suit but held a glass of wine in one hand.

"They gave me an interview at the end," Baron replied.

Richard checked his watch. "We'll be sure to turn on the TV at six."

Baron smiled, but a little sadly. For the first time, he didn't deserve the accolades. The clock was ticking down. The things he had done would catch up to him. He wouldn't be on the team long enough to have earned the celebration. But none of his family knew that. Not yet.

Tonya turned to her cousin Deb's son. "But back to what we were talking about, Chad. This incident isn't going to be counted against your probation, is it? Will this affect your ability to be confirmed on the police department?"

Chad Rauch stared at his beer bottle. "God, I hope not. I only just got signed off by my field training officer."

Baron slid a Ritz cracker off his sister's plate and dipped it in the creamy white sauce. "What happened?"

Instead of answering, Chad continued to stare at his beer, his face turning warm pink.

Regina offered the explanation for him. "His key to the police station went missing."

Chad sighed through puffed cheeks. "No, it was stolen. It had to have been. I just can't think how. Then somebody used it to break into the PD and attacked one of the telecommunicators..." He raked his hands through his hair. "I've been wracking my brains, thinking over every contact I made with the public that day. I just can't think how it could have... Did I drop it?"

Baron looked Chad in the eye. "I'm really sorry, man."

Chad merely leaned his chin in his palm and shook his head. Of course, he had no way of knowing what Baron really meant. He was sorry for lifting the key card and putting Chad into this position. Such a simple thing, to slip it out of his jacket pocket two nights ago. And yet the regret sat in Baron's soul like a well, the bottom so far from the surface that the water swirled inky black. But Baron had already laid a thick layer of ice over the top. He couldn't afford to get hung up by the profoundness of his regret. Chad had no idea the depths of the game Baron was navigating. There had been no other way... Chad would understand. One day. A long, long time from now.

Tonya reached across the counter and patted Chad's arm. "It'll be fine. You made a mistake, but this doesn't have to be the end."

Chad nodded miserably. "It's just hard."

"Harder makes you stronger," Richard said.

Chad flashed him a smile, then forced himself to sit up a little taller. "Yes, sir."

Richard lifted his wine glass toward him. "Atta boy. You've got this."

Harder makes you stronger. Another Hackett family mantra. Baron held it in his mind. He'd need it to help him endure the road ahead.

Tonya scraped her caramelized onions over a platter of steaks, steaming and stewing in juices. "Let's not dwell on it. New topic. Deb, you have no idea how much we owe you for recommending Lake Geneva when we decided to leave LA. Reggie just needed someplace quiet to focus on school until graduation..."

Baron's mom and her cousin chattered on about Lake Geneva and everything it had to offer—not least of which, more privacy for the Hackett family. A privacy Baron was about to ruin again. He studied his parents' happy faces. They would understand. They would see why he did what he did. They would support him, like always.

Just as they were trooping to the dinner table with serving dishes piled high, the phone rang in its cradle on the kitchen counter.

"I'll get it," Baron said. He put down the salad and picked up the phone as the rest of the family moved into the dining room. "Hello?"

A female voice replied. "Hello. May I speak with Baron Hackett, please?"

He didn't recognize the voice, and yet something cold twisted in his stomach. In his soul, he knew this was it. The clock had ticked down to zero. But he would have turned himself in anyway if the wait had dragged on too long. "This is Baron," he replied.

"My name is Special Agent Emory Mullins," the woman went on. "I'm with the Wisconsin Department of Criminal Investigations. I was told you might have some information that could help with a case I'm working on."

She was told he had information? Not that he was a suspect? An interesting angle—one Baron hadn't anticipated. But in a heartbeat, he adjusted to the tactic. It made sense. They wanted information. They assumed he would be reluctant to give it to them, and thus they would "lure" him in by suggesting he was only a witness and not a suspect.

On one point, they had miscalculated. He was more than ready to give them information.

"How can I help you?" Baron asked.

"Would you be willing to meet me at the Lake Geneva Police Department for an interview?"

"Yes. When?"

"I can meet you in an hour."

Baron checked the clock on the kitchen wall—a sheet of glass with silver hands, no numerals. It was five P.M. Agent Mullins was working overtime and they wanted him in fast. Because they were that sure he was their man? Because they knew his dad's lawyer could make the drive from Chicago in ninety minutes?

"I'll be there," Baron replied. And the lawyer wouldn't. The man would have a heart attack if he knew what Baron was about to do.

"Great," the woman said. "Just tell them at the PD lobby that you're there to meet Agent Mullins. They'll show you where to go."

"Will do."

"Thank you. See you in an hour."

"See you in an hour." And then the wait would be over. The anxiety in his chest could be released.

Baron hung up. He inhaled slowly and let it all out, then followed his family into the dining area.

"Did you bring the salad, honey?" his mom asked.

Instead of answering, Baron looked at her and his father. "Mom, Dad, can I talk to you? Privately?"

"Of course." His dad set down the water pitcher with which he'd been filling glasses. "What is it?"

Baron met his parents' gazes steadily. "I've gotta tell you something."

CHAPTER FIFTEEN
MONICA

I plugged a key into a metal plate mounted to the wall outside the interview room door. "You know how these work," I said to Agent Emory Mullins. "Just turn to the right and the video will start recording."

"Got it." Mullins' auburn hair was trimmed in a practical boy cut. She wore a navy two-piece suit and no jewelry. Minimal makeup—just a touch of mascara. She was all business. I liked her. I pulled the key from the switch and handed it to Mullins, who put it in her pocket.

We stood in the middle of the secured waiting room, a cluster of chairs sitting by racks of literature—help for domestic violence, self-defense classes, McGruff the Crime Dog. "Coffee and water are through that door in the break room," I went on. "Give the door a tug and Angie will let you through." Like all the doors in the station, the telecommunicators had control via a switch panel at their desk. "Vending machine's right here, if he wants a snack."

"Sounds good."

I glanced up and down the waiting room and tapped my foot, wondering if I was forgetting anything. Any minute, Baron Hackett would walk through the door. Nerves raced up and down my spine. Finally, I'd know what kind of kid he was: a model young citizen, or a petty criminal who broke into locked buildings and attacked anyone who got in his way. Hopefully, I'd also find out whether he was working for Sergeant Horace Stubbs. I could feel the truth churning in my gut. Stubbs wanted those records destroyed. He'd found the most unlikely kid to do it. He'd crafted what he thought was the perfect crime. My fists clenched and loosened at the thought of finally seeing the man behind bars where he belonged.

"Anything else you need?" I asked.

Agent Mullins shook her head. "I think that'll do. Thanks for letting me use your facility."

I shrugged. "Any time." In fact, I was delighted. This was officially Mullins' case, not mine due to that conflict of interest problem. I wouldn't have any part in the interview or in following up with clues that may be revealed. But at least I'd be close to the action.

The door from the lobby buzzed open and a young man walked through. I stood a little straighter, nostrils flaring, a dog on alert. This was him, I knew it. Baron

Hackett. My eyes scanned up and down, mining for clues. He was tall. Muscular. Of course. Quarterback. For the occasion, he'd dressed casual yet smart: khaki shorts and a striped polo shirt, royal blue and white. His dark hair was styled in a carefree, windblown look. A diamond stud glittered in one ear and a cowrie shell necklace hung around his neck. He looked every bit the accomplished yet popular boy all of Badger High was in love with.

"Hello," he said, shoulders square, his presentation completely on-point. "I'm looking for Agent Mullins."

"That's me." Mullins shook his hand. "Thanks for coming in. Is there anything I can get you before we start? Water? Coffee? Need anything to eat?"

Baron shook his head. "I'm good, thank you. I'm ready whenever you are."

"Perfect." Mullins nodded toward the interview room. "C'mon in and make yourself at home."

Baron strode through the door. Before following him in, Mullins plugged the key I'd given her into the switch and turned it to the right. Then she stepped into the room and closed the door behind her.

I spun on my heel, hip-checked the lock on the door to the break room, and made for the stairwell; the elevator was too slow for my patience levels. I took the steps two at a time and coursed down the hall to the detective bureau. At my own desk, I threw myself into my chair and grabbed for my computer mouse. Something soft and squishy filled my hand instead—the foam stress trout Lehman had given me. I batted it aside and found my mouse a few inches away. I woke up my computer. The video software was already open on my screen. I parked a set of headphones over my ears and hit play. After a second of blackness, the screen filled with a bird's-eye view of the interview room downstairs.

Baron Hackett sat on one side of the gray, Formica-topped table, the camera pointed toward his face. Agent Mullins sat opposite him.

"Address?" Mullins was saying, her hand moving across a notebook on the table in front of her. She was still gathering the basics. Baron provided the answers one-by-one as she requested them. When she was done, she leaned back in her chair. "Thanks, Baron." She crossed her legs and laced her fingers around her knee, by all appearances ready to start the interview proper.

But Baron spoke up first. "I think you're looking for this." He reached into a cargo pocket on his shorts and laid something small, white, and rectangular on the table.

A key card.

I sat upright in my chair, pulse racing.

Mullins stared at the key card, lips parted. She was off her game. I could see it. Baron was in here based off an anonymous tip—a junk tip, as the majority of them were. She hadn't anticipated a confession. And first thing in the interview? Unheard of.

But she only froze for a beat before switching gears smoothly. "Can you explain where you got that?"

"My second cousin, Chad Rauch, is an officer with the Lake Geneva Police Department," Baron replied. "I took it from his jacket pocket on June 9th, two days ago. Then I used it to break into the police station that same night."

I shifted an eyebrow at him. *You cocky bastard.* So that was Baron's type: the attention whore. Winning awards wasn't good enough for him. He wanted renown, for good deeds or evil. He wanted the world to know what he'd done. What he was capable of.

I leaned back and tapped a finger on my chin. So our hapless rookie, Chad Rauch, was Baron Hackett's cousin. Correction: second cousin. That's how I'd missed the connection despite all my research. I hadn't thought to look up distantly related family. I snarled to myself. Stupid oversight. I'd do better next time.

To her credit, Mullins was now taking everything in stride. She didn't so much as unlace her fingers. "Baron, it's my duty to inform you that you are now under arrest."

"I understand," he replied.

"You have the right to remain silent..." she proceeded with the rest of the Miranda warning.

I clasped my hands in front of my mouth like an eager, finger-biting prayer. This was it. We'd gotten him. The person who had attacked Steph Buchanan. Steph and her family would be relieved. The entire police department could relax. We'd avenged our pack member. Sent another low-life piece of shit to jail. I wished I knew who had called in with that anonymous tip. This one had been golden. Nail on the head. I'd like to personally thank the girl. But I'd probably never know who it was.

"Do you understand these rights as I have explained them to you?" Mullins concluded.

"I do."

"Do you waive the right to have an attorney present during questioning?"

"Yes. And I'd like the chance to speak freely before you proceed with your own questions."

Mullins waved a hand. "Go ahead." She'd be an idiot to turn him down. He was on a roll and there was no bean he wouldn't spill.

But I frowned. Something was wrong. He was so... *polite.* There was no pride. No boasting. He wasn't acting like an attention junkie. He could be on the Autism spectrum, but I wasn't convinced of that yet. What was this, then? A need to unload? But that didn't feel right, either. I stared intently into Baron's face, desperate to understand. His features remained calm, smooth. He could have been taking an interview regarding a job for which he knew he was well-qualified. I leaned an elbow on my knee and chewed a nail. He was one up on me. I hated this.

"First, I apologize for any wrongs I've done," Baron proceeded, "and any harm I may have caused. I needed a particular set of records. Records pertaining to a former LGPD officer, Sergeant Horace Stubbs."

This was it, the part where Baron admitted he was working for Stubbs. That Stubbs was desperate to clean up a dirty past. To not only lock Roger Holland up but to throw away the key. I tasted sweet victory. I fixed my eyes on Baron Hackett and waited for it.

"My only goal was to prove the innocence of a man who has been serving time for a murder he never committed. Roger Holland."

My jaw fell loose. Wait, what? As I sat gaping, the leg-up Baron had on me expanded into a decisive lead and I was eating his dust.

"Please explain," Mullins said.

"On August 29, 1995, Roger Holland was arrested for supposedly murdering his friend, Kent Bullinger. The arresting officer was Sergeant Horace Stubbs. But another officer present that day, Officer Monica Steele, filed a written complaint against Stubbs, suggesting that he had altered crime scene evidence to make the death appear as a murder, not an accident. No one ever followed up o n Officer Steele's complaint. Holland went to trial for murder and was convicted and has been behind bars ever since."

I stared at Baron Hackett. What was happening?

Mullins tapped her pen on her notepad. "Do you realize you're raising very serious allegations against an officer of the law?"

Instead of answering, Hackett pulled a paper from his pocket and unfolded it on the table. "Here's a copy of the complaint that was filed by Officer Steele. Until now, I believe no one ever laid eyes on it, besides Steele and her lieutenant at the time, Theodore Townsend. On the morning of June 10th, I mailed the original to Roger Holland's attorney. My guess is that he'll use it to demand a retrial."

I stared at the screen, my mind and my emotions a total blank. This wasn't about Stubbs covering his ass. It wasn't about Baron being the hired grunt. Baron was—

Baron was me. The over-achiever. The whistle-blower. The one small voice bent on seeing real justice done, whatever the cost. I couldn't approve of his methods. I never would. And yet in a weird way, we were on the same side. It twisted my soul into a pretzel to try to wrap my mind around it.

I bowed my head over my desk and massaged my temples. Well, this was why we'd handed the case over to D.C.I. Completely drunk on bias and revenge, I'd refused to consider other possibilities. Damn idiot.

Mullins leaned forward and glanced over the report. "How did you know this document even existed?"

"I work with Roger Holland's granddaughter, Melissa Kraft. The family has always maintained that Roger was innocent. That he'd never kill his best friend. Melissa's mother claims that at the time of Roger Holland's trial, Officer Steele implied that the trial was somehow unlawful. That another officer was to blame."

I closed my eyes and groaned. I'd forgotten all about that. I'd been furious that the case had been allowed to proceed to trial. In a moment of unscrupulous rage, I'd let something slip. *It's not your dad's fault; it's Stubbs'.* Something to that effect. No doubt it had given the family hope. But of course, they'd never had any evidence. None of us had.

Mullins picked the document up and read it more carefully, the report I had crafted so passionately as a young cop. The one that had branded me as an idiot back in the day. When she was finished, she turned to Baron once again. "So you broke into the Lake Geneva Police Department to steal this written complaint. You did it to try to exonerate a prisoner. Did you also attack a police department employee who arrived on the scene to investigate your break-in?"

Baron flexed his jaw. His eyes saddened, yet refused to look away from Agent Mullins. "It was an accident. I had what I'd come for. I was leaving. Then I saw the woman in the hallway. I stopped to decide what to do. But I bumped a board that was leaning against a wall. It hit her on the back of the head. I made sure she was breathing comfortably, then I left the building. I never meant to hurt anyone."

Mullins looked at him dubiously. "Why, Baron? Why break into a police station? Why take the risk? The risk of being intercepted, the risk of being caught. You didn't even know Roger Holland." She glanced over her notes. "You weren't even born at the time of his incarceration."

I knew his answer before he spoke it. I knew it because I'd said the exact same thing to my then-husband. *Why are you doing this, Monica?* he had pleaded with me. We'd only just bought the picture frames for the snapshots of us being sworn into office. He knew as well as I did that blowing the whistle on my superior, a man who had the favor of his own superior, could spell the end of my fledgling career. That was back when we'd actually cared about each other.

Baron put his finger on the paper between him and Agent Mullins. "This complaint has been sitting in the LGPD's storage room for eighteen years. At least one person still working for the department knew it was there. And yet she never did anything about it, even when the people who previously stood in her way were retired. For eighteen years, an innocent man has been in jail while the guilty one walks free." Baron stared deeply into Agent Mullins' eyes. "I did it because—"

I said it with him. "—no one else had the guts to do the right thing."

I closed my eyes and remembered the way my ex had looked at me. The understanding. The acceptance. The unspoken promise that he would stand by my side, no matter the blowback. And he had. Of course, that had been a lifetime ago, another world ago, and God only knew where he was now. Maybe rotting in hell, like I often hoped he was. But at the time, his support had meant everything to me.

I let Baron's accusations soak in. I was the one who'd let that piece of paper languish in storage while Holland languished in jail. I'd tried to raise Cain at first, but Lieutenant Townsend had hushed it all down. Laughed at "how little I knew." Implied I was a dumb female. That maybe I shouldn't wear the badge. Law enforcement was a man's world—more blatantly then than it was now. I'd gone from fighting for an innocent man to fighting for my own right to be on the police department.

Baron and Mullins' interview rolled on, as I knew it would for hours. I would listen to every minute, even though it felt like stabbing needles into my chest. I should have fought harder for Roger Holland. Instead, I'd unwittingly left it to a teenager to finish the work I'd abandoned, and to do it in a way that had harmed one of our own telecommunicators. It sickened me to admit it;

I owed it to Baron Hackett for finally setting the record straight. Holland's. Stubbs'. My own.

He was going to prison for this. There was no question. He'd still broken into a police station, stolen police property, and injured a police department employee, intentionally or otherwise. Due to the seriousness of the offense, he might even be tried as an adult, which would carry with it stiffer penalties. Maybe the judge would show lenience, take into account Baron's motives and absence of any prior record. But the fact remained: he was giving up his freedom for someone else's. When Holland had first been arrested, I had acted all tough. But when the going got hard, I'd faltered. I utterly lacked Baron's kind of courage. When it came down to Holland's freedom or my badge, I'd chosen my badge.

My eyes filled with angry tears. Angry with myself. With my failure. My eye found the rainbow trout on the corner of my desk—*Gone Fishin'*. I grabbed it and flung it across the room.

WEDNESDAY, JUNE 12, 2013

Chapter Sixteen
BAILEY

I guess watching the same nature documentary three times in a row is pretty lame. But I was alone, like always. My foster dad was at his restaurant—he never quit working—and this was one of my favorite films ever. Penguins are so freaking adorable. And to be honest, I wasn't actually watching it. I was just trying not to cry. It was my day off, which meant there was nothing to distract me. To keep me from thinking. So I had banned myself from thinking. At all. About anything.

And that's how I found myself waddling up and down the snow-packed Antarctic, fluffing up my down and feeling utterly amazed that my webbed feet weren't even cold. Because I was a freaking penguin.

How close had I come to making the team? Like, really close? Not close at all? Did it matter? No. Because I *hadn't* made the team. An inch or a mile, it was all the same.

Oh, damn it, I was thinking. I stared hard at the penguins jumping off the sea ice like little tuxedoed torpedoes. I needed to be a penguin. There were anchovies out there. Lots of delicious, fat little anchovies...

My phone rang on the end table. I don't think I heard it the first two or three times. When I finally did, I had a panicked feeling—my non-penguin subconscious screaming at me—that there was only one ring left. I glanced at the screen. It said *Robb Landis*, my boss. Why would he be calling? I should probs pick it up. Like, before my phone sent him to voice mail.

"Hello?"

"Hey, Bailey, it's Robb. Say, we have a little problem. Turns out one of our mail jumpers... ah... Well, he won't be on the team this year."

"Oh, really?" My brain was still catching tiny silver fish somewhere off the coast of South America. Swarming in breathtaking synchronization with my fellow penguins. Wrapping that school of delicious little pizza toppers into an ever-tightening ball. Darting into their midst and filling my beak with squirming, life-giving meat.

I hate anchovies on pizza.

"Yeah," Robb babbled on. "So the judges and I had a quick meeting, and we've decided... Well, we'd like you to take the opening."

I picked off a squirming, oily little fish and swallowed it whole. I'd grab as many more as I could stuff into my belly, then swim back to the colony and puke it all up for the adorable little fluff-puffin squawking its tiny head off back at the nest.

Wait... What had Robb just said?

"You want... you want *me* to be on the mail jumping team?"

"That's right." Robb sounded like he was smiling. Like he enjoyed making someone's dearest wish come true. Like he was the guy who shows up at your front door with a check the size of a small marine research boat.

My brain was stuck halfway between Lake Geneva and the Antarctic. "Me?" I asked again, like I'd been swimming in ice-strewn waters too long and gotten a brain freeze.

Robb laughed. "Yes, Bailey. We'd like you to be on the mail jumping team this summer. Can you be at the Mailboat at seven Saturday morning?"

I finally realized I wasn't a penguin. *I was a mail jumper.* "Yes!" I squeaked, for all the world like a hungry fluff-puffin. "Yes, I'll be there!"

"Great! Thanks a million, Bailey. I'll shoot you an email with the rest of your schedule."

"Yes, sir. Thank you, sir."

He laughed. "Not a problem. Thanks for helping us out, Bailey."

We hung up.

I dropped my phone. It vanished somewhere into the depths of the lay-z-boy recliner. I clapped both hands over my mouth. Squeezed my eyes shut. Tried not to scream.

I was a mail jumper.

And then came the tears.

I was a mail jumper. I'd get to work with Tommy. Like, almost every day all summer long. Maybe for once I'd feel like I wasn't completely alone in the world. Maybe I'd feel like someone was actually there for me. Someone who got nervous for you when you were about to do something daring. Someone who helped you recite your lines when you had no idea what you were doing.

For once—finally—something good had happened in my life.

I got up from the chair, stretched my arms wide, and spun in circles. My belly happy and full of fish, I twirled all the way home through crystal-blue waters to the colony and a hungry little fluff-puffin.

SATURDAY, JUNE 15, 2013

CHAPTER SEVENTEEN

TOMMY

A s I walked down the pier that Saturday morning,
there was Bailey sitting on the bow of the Mailboat,
feet dangling over the water, heels rocking back and forth.
She had arrived even before me, and that was saying
something.

I grinned. My last-minute mail jumper. Robb had
called a couple nights ago with the change in plans. "That's
fine," I'd said, heating up soup over the stove while Cubs
vs. Reds played on the radio. "Tell her to wear something
that dries fast."

He laughed. We hung up. I turned off the soup and
leaned on the stovetop, staring at the backsplash and
smiling like a damned old fool. Bailey-girl. She'd made the
team. Ten minutes went by before I realized the ball game
was over and the Cubs had lost. It didn't matter. Bailey was
gonna be a mail jumper.

"Morning," I called as I got closer to the boat. She was dressed in navy shorts, a white tee shirt with the cruise line logo, and a pair of running shoes. Her ponytail hung over her shoulder and her fly-away hair haloed her face, almost honey-blond in the morning sun.

"Morning!" She jumped down from the boat, landed on the dock, and bounced on her toes, her hands clasped behind her back. Looking at her now, so young and eager and innocent as a new-born day, it was hard to believe what she'd done. She'd called the police and turned in Baron Hackett. I didn't know that from her or Robb or Chief Wade Erickson or anybody; I simply knew it. What else could explain Baron's absence, Bailey's presence, Robb's hushed admission that Baron had apparently gotten into some trouble with the law? As inconceivable as it was that Baron could be the guilty party, it was even more stunning to me that Bailey, my shy little clamshell, had been courageous enough to report him.

It would take a while to wrap my mind around the whole thing. But in the meantime, one fact was immutable: Bailey stuck her neck out to do the right, hard thing and ended up a mail jumper. While Baron's alleged crimes unsettled me on many levels, I guess I was okay with the outcome.

More than that. Something swelled in my chest like the lake before a storm. Pride. I hadn't felt that since my son had graduated college; gotten a solid job; swept his way up the corporate ladder to higher echelons of responsibility. I'd never told him how I felt. I wasn't sure I had the words to tell Bailey, either.

"What do you need me to do?" She grinned brightly, her cheeks flushed pink as if she'd run laps on the piers to burn off energy. She was clearly eager to begin her duties as a Lake Geneva mail jumper.

I hid my smile by bowing my head as I stuck my key in the lock. When I spoke, my voice adopted my old tone of a petty officer second class. "Grab some paper towels and wipe down these windows." I held the door open for her. "I want 'em all gleaming."

"Yes, sir!" Before I could remind her not to call me *sir*, she shot inside the boat and bee-lined for the cleaning closet in the aft.

I watched her go, shaking my head, then gazed over the lake. The water was azure blue and smooth as glass except where a family of ducks raised a few ripples below the boats. The sand grooming machine chugged along the nearby swimming beach, the operator whistling a little Frank Sinatra, one of my favorites, "That's Life." The trees along the shore were in full leaf, promising another glorious Lake Geneva summer full of laughter, cannon balls, and ice cream cones.

I sighed. This was going to be a good year.

I stepped into the boat to join my new mail jumper.

MONDAY, JUNE 17, 2013

Chapter Eighteen

SKULL

Leaning against a tree, a narrow man in ratty black jeans and a hoodie watched the door of the Walworth County Judicial Center. With the sleeves ripped off his sweater, his tanned arms were bared to the sun, along with his favorite tattoo—the rose-schadel, a skull with a rose painted on its cracked white temple.

He checked his watch. The sentencing hearing couldn't take more than a few minutes. There had never even been a trial. No need. Baron had confessed to everything, leaving the judge nothing to do but decide how long to lock him up and how big a fine to leave for his rich-ass dad to pay.

The glass doors swung open and the man of the hour strode through. Baron Hackett walked tall and proud, dressed in a two-piece suit but flanked by sheriff's deputies. The boy's hands were cuffed behind his back. It was only a short stroll from here to the waiting squad car and a short ride from Walworth County to the juvenile detention facility in Racine.

As Baron and his guards passed, Skull tilted his head over a cigarette and lighter, letting his cupped hands and his hood conceal his face. Over his fingers, he glanced at the kid. They exchanged a look, nothing more. But in the brief moment their eyes met, Skull sent his thanks.

Their scheme had worked. The boy was taking the fall. Skull was going free. Baron hadn't done a thing besides lift his cousin's key card. Well, that and devise the alibi, the whole Stubbs-Holland angle. Genius bit of work, that was. *We've got to throw them a bone,* Baron had insisted. *Divert attention from what we're really after.* Lucky thing the kid had an inside scoop on that old, forgotten murder case. It was just the thing they'd needed. Skull had rifled the Stubbs-Holland papers while leaving the ones they were really after untouched. The original documents were safe and sound back at the police station, but their information locked away in Skull's brain.

Skull was free to move forward with the plan now. Meanwhile, Baron could assume all responsibility for the break-in while still looking like a bleeding saint. The incident with the police dispatcher had been an unlucky complication—Skull had seen no other way of escape but to crack her in the back of the head with one of the boards leaning against the wall. But Baron had managed to smooth even that one over, framing it as an accident. The kid was confident he wouldn't be behind bars long. He'd win the system over with his impeccable good behavior. Skull wasn't sure if the boy was brave or just stupid. Either way, Baron's sacrifice served his purposes.

And The Man's.

After all, it wasn't Skull whom Baron was trying to impress.

The sheriff's deputies tucked Baron away in the back seat, reminding him to watch his head. They got in the front. Closed the doors. Took off down the street in the direction of Racine.

Skull pulled his phone out of his pocket. He dialed a number he didn't keep in his contacts. A number he'd erase from his call history as soon as the conversation was over.

It rang once. The Man picked up. "Yes?"

Skull savored his anticipation. Took a drag from the cigarette. "It's all taken care of."

"You have the information?"

"Yep. You were right. The cops had a whole folder on the Markham Ring." Seventeen years ago, the Ring had gone down in a blaze of glory. Bobby Markham and his boys were caught red-handed in an alley behind the last bank they ever broke into, right in their home town of Lake Geneva. Bobby never lived to see the morrow.

"And?" The Man prodded.

Skull took another deep breath through the cigarette and blew a long column of smoke. "I know where to find Fritz." He let the words hang, knowing The Man's eagerness was coming into full blossom on the other end of the line. "The Plan can move forward."

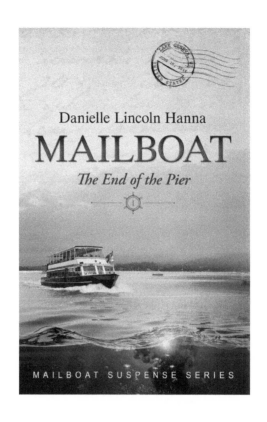

Danielle Lincoln Hanna

MAILBOAT

The End of the Pier

MAILBOAT SUSPENSE SERIES

All she wanted was a family of her own. Instead, she found a body at the end of the pier...

FREE EBOOK!

You Could Be Reading My Next Book As I Write It!

Patreon is a website where top fans can support their favorite creatives in exchange for exclusive benefits. My Patrons get to read my chapters the minute they're out of my pen.

Beyond that, every chapter comes with Book Club Questions, which have prompted some amazing, uplifting conversations. (Good vibes only in my online spaces!) I also post Behind-the-Scenes info, revealing what went into the creation of the story, and the thoughts going through my heart and soul as I write.

My Patrons get a more intimate experience than any other fan. So, come aboard! This is a cruise unlike any you've experienced before.

Join Us Today!

BENEATH THE SURFACE
"DID YOU GROW UP IN LAKE GENEVA?"

I've been asked many times whether I grew up in Lake Geneva, Wisconsin. I've also been asked whether I worked for the Lake Geneva Cruise Line. And, of course, I've been asked whether I was ever a Lake Geneva mail jumper.

The answers to those questions are no, no, and no. I'm extremely flattered, however, that even life-long residents of this lakeside community are convinced I must be a local. (Why, thank you. I'm just really into my research.)

As a matter of fact, I grew up in Mandan, North Dakota, over seven hundred miles away from the lake with the crystal-clear water. I've worked a variety of jobs, from waitress to quilt shop clerk to animal caretaker at a humane society. (Or as I like to say, a Canine and Feline Waste Management Specialist.)

But I was only ever a mail jumper for a day, and that was to do research for this series. Before the advent of this story, I had never so much as heard of Lake Geneva, Wisconsin.

At this point in the conversation, my readers will invariably scratch their heads and ask, "Then... how did you end up writing these books?"

Well, it was all thanks to a series of coincidences. In fact, I like to say that the Mailboat came and found me.

The date was November 4, 2009, and I was bored. I get this particularly pernicious kind of boredom in which all I want to do is dash out a breathtaking work of staggering genius. Unfortunately, writing doesn't work that way. You have to write your first draft first—also known as the "sloppy copy"—and then you have to rewrite it maybe twenty times before it comes anywhere near the hallowed realms of staggering genius.

So that afternoon, already knowing that anything I dashed out would be basically a load of garbage, I didn't try. I didn't want garbage, I wanted *genius!* So I aimed for the next best thing: Seeing if anyone *else* had put out a breathtaking work of staggering genius lately. Something new. Something unusual. Something to send my brain off into waves of creative ecstasy.

Since I'd already read everything on my own bookshelves, I turned on the television.

You read that right. I started flipping channels. I think you can guess how well *that* was likely to work. Hard enough finding something entertaining, never mind genius.

But that afternoon in November was the first and only time surfing channels for genius actually worked.

This was when the series of coincidences fell into place. While we do have our own public television station in North Dakota, we also air Minnesota Public Television. (I have no idea why.) And while Minnesota has plenty of its own excellent programming, they also carry some from Wisconsin. (Again, no idea why.) One of the programs they carried was a show called *Outdoor Wisconsin*.

And for whatever reason, on that particular afternoon, that particular show decided to rebroadcast a segment they'd originally recorded some *thirteen years* previously. (Thirteen years? I mean... why?)

But it just so happened that this segment was about the Lake Geneva Mailboat.

Let me paint the picture: There I was, flipping channels, when the image of a lake, a boat, and a young lady jumping on and off the boat filled my screen. I paused, thumb hovering over the remote, and tilted my head, puppy-dog style. What was I seeing? I watched as she put mail in a box on a pier, then ran to get back on board the still-moving vessel. The boat was full of tourists, who cheered when she landed a particularly challenging jump, and listened attentively as she and the captain narrated a tour of the history of the summer resort lake.

I watched the segment through to the end, eyes wide and jaw slack. For once in my life, surfing channels had actually resulted in me landing on a staggering work of breathtaking genius. When the segment was done, I turned off the TV and walked away.

"That's it!" I said aloud to an empty room. "I don't need to see anything else today."

By the time I'd left the room, the three main elements of my brand-new story were already clear in my mind: The main character would be a young mail jumper. Another vital player would be the Mailboat captain. And the problem for them both would be a body at the end of a pier...

Did you enjoy this glimpse beneath the surface?
JOIN ME ON PATREON

ACKNOWLEDGMENTS

S ince I started writing the Mailboat Suspense Series, I've pictured snapshots of Bailey's life before she became a Lake Geneva mail jumper. Recently, I was inspired to capture one of those snapshots as a story (this one). In addition to exploring Bailey and Monica's lives, I was eager to reveal more of Tommy the way he was before the events of the main series took place. From Book One on, events unravel so quickly that I felt the reader never got a chance to see the relationship Bailey and Tommy had early on. I hope any curiosities have now been satisfied. As for Ryan... he's still a sergeant in Minneapolis, breaking womens' hearts and getting his tires slashed.

Even this short book wouldn't have been possible without the help of many friends. My thanks, as always, to the Lake Geneva Cruise Line (https://www.cruiselakegeneva.com/), operators of the real-life Lake Geneva Mailboat. Thank you for the inspiration. Gratitude specifically to *General Managers Harold Friestad (ret.)* and *Jack Lothian*, to *the Mailboat Captain Neill Frame*, and to *Office Manager Ellen Burling*.

I'm forever grateful to my expert advisers and the time they freely give to help me write better, more accurate stories. *Lieutenant Edward Gritzner, Sergeant Jason Hall*, and *Telecommunicator Rita Moore* of the Lake Geneva Police Department, thank you for explaining how an internal investigation would be handled, sharing tales of the old days when your dads and granddads were policing, and divulging that delicious detail about the "haunted doors" to the maintenance room. (Priceless.) *Sam Petitto* (retired police officer), thanks for your long emails brimming with information on crime databases and other topics that would bore most readers (but not me). *David Congdon* (Threat Assessment and Countermeasures Specialist), I can't express how much I appreciate our conversations on psychology and why on earth my characters do what they do.

To my long-time brainstorming partner, *Carrie Lynn Lewis*, thanks for helping me get unstuck on a particularly tricky detail. To my writer's club, *We Write Good*, thanks for being the first eyes on my manuscript and saving me from embarrassing myself with words I must have written while sleeping.

My dedicated and hard-working Early Reader Team read this book prior to publication and provided their comments, critiques, and corrections: *Susan Beatty, Stephanie Brancati, Kathy Collins, David Congdon, Brenda Dahlfors, Beth Dancy, Loranda Daniels Buoy, Nancy Diestler, Lynda Fergus, Pat Gerber, Lt. Edward Gritzner, Sgt. Jason Hall, Lynn Hirshman, Michelle Love, Steven Maresso, Lisa McCann, Elaine Montgomery, T/C Rita Moore, Rebecca Paciorek, Linda Pautz, Sam Petitto (ret. police officer), Sanda Putnam, JoAnn Schutte, Kathy Skorstad, Judy Tucker, Kimberly Wade, Carol D. Westover,* and *Mary-Jane Woodward.* Many thanks for your sharp eyes!

Thanks to *Matt Mason Photography* (www.MattMasonPhotography.com) for the photo of the Mailboat that became the front cover, *W. J. Goes* for escorting my photography crew around the lake in his Boston whaler, and *Maryna Zhukova of MaryDes* (www.MaryDes.eu) for the cover design. Maryna, I'm happy this one was your favorite. All your covers are my favorite.

Rebecca Paciorek, Susan Beatty, and *JoAnn Schwartz Schutte* of Blue Dot Marketing (http://rpaciorek8.wixsite.com/bluedotdigitalmkt), you are the best promotions team an author could ask for.

A big thanks to *my readers* for supporting my writing habit. When I put up the pre-order for this book—with no cover art and no book description—you stepped right up and asked for your copies. Thank you for believing in me that much. I am grateful and deeply respect the fact that you trust your leisure hours to me.

Finally, thanks to *Fergus* my black cat for hogging half the pillow every night (and purring in my ear). Thanks to my German Shepherd *Angel* for finally outgrowing the puppy phase. Actually, I love you. You are such a good girl. And thanks to my boyfriend *Charles William Maclay* for holding me up when I'm tired, holding my hand on our walks, and holding my heart for always.

BOOKS BY DANIELLE LINCOLN HANNA

The Mailboat Suspense Series

The Girl on the Boat: A Prequel Novella

Mailboat I: The End of the Pier

Mailboat II: The Silver Helm

Mailboat III: The Captain's Tale

Mailboat IV: The Shift in the Wind

Mailboat V: The End of Summer

Mailboat VI: *coming soon*

DanielleLincolnHanna.com/ShopNow

ABOUT THE AUTHOR

Danielle Lincoln Hanna is the author of the Mailboat Suspense Series. While she now lives in the Rocky Mountains of Montana, her first love is still the Great Plains of North Dakota where she was born. When she's not writing, you can find her hiking with her boyfriend Charles, adventuring with her German Shepherd Angel, and avoiding surprise attacks from her cat Fergus.

CARL JEUNE

THE IT BOOK

PALMETTO
PUBLISHING
Charleston, SC
www.PalmettoPublishing.com

The It Book

First Edition

Hardcover ISBN: 979-8-8229-3971-4
Paperback ISBN: 979-8-8229-3972-1

DEDICATION

TO MY FAMILY, I am eternally grateful for the love that fills our hearts and the connection that binds us together. It is a privilege to have you by my side, and I will forever cherish the moments we have shared. My extended family, your love and support have made me feel connected to a larger community. The memories we have created together are treasured, and the bonds we share remain strong, despite the miles that may separate us. Thank you for being my family, my biggest cheerleaders, and my greatest source of love and happiness. I am so fortunate to call you my own.

TO STEPHANI none of this would be possible without your effort and sacrifices

TO MY MOTHER, *VIOLA*,
Sometimes it takes losing someone to truly appreciate and realize their significance in our lives. Losing you made me understand just how much you mean to me. Now that I've found you again, I promise to cherish and value our connection every single day.

CONTENTS

INTRODUCTION

Through the pages of this book, I hope to shed light on the harsh realities that are often overshadowed by the hustle and bustle of day-to-day life. Growing up in the concrete jungle taught me how to navigate the treacherous paths and make difficult choices just to survive. But as I struggled to find my place in this unforgiving world, I realized that there is more to life than mere survival. With each passing day, I learned valuable lessons and gained a deeper understanding of the human experience.

Writing this book has allowed me to reflect on my journey, to explore the depths of my own thoughts and emotions. It is through these words that I hope to bring my experiences to life and make a genuine connection with those who need them the most. In the darkness of the concrete jungle, I discovered a flicker of light. And now, I offer that light to you, dear reader. May this book be a beacon of hope, a source of inspiration, and a guide through the complexities of life.

May every word I write resonate with your soul, reminding you that you are not alone on this journey. Together, we can rise above our circumstances and find meaning amidst the chaos.

Let these pages be a reminder that there is beauty in the struggle, strength in vulnerability, and wisdom in reflection. May my words provide solace in moments of doubt, encouragement in times of despair, and guidance when the path ahead seems unclear. I wrote this book not for myself, but for you. May it be a lifeline, a source of comfort, and a catalyst for change. And as you embark on your own journey, may you find the courage to share your own story, to impact and connect with those who may need it. May the words I write transcend the pages, reaching out to souls in need, reminding them that they, too, have a voice worth sharing.

Throughout the pages, you will come across thought-provoking questions. These queries are designed to make you pause and consider their purpose and relevance in your own life. Delve into these questions and explore how their answers can be applied to your unique circumstances. Use them as opportunities for self-reflection and as catalysts for positive change.

THE ALPHA MALE

...consumed with the need to feel good that we might kill ourselves in the process.

Humans have a natural inclination to label things as it helps them make sense of the world around them. When people have a shared understanding of certain labels, they can effectively convey information and ideas to one another. Labels act as a shorthand that encapsulates meaning and reduces ambiguity, enabling efficient and clear communication. For instance, labels like "apple," "chair," or "book" allow individuals to refer to these objects without having to provide lengthy descriptions each time. Overall, the human need to label things arises from the desire to understand, communicate, remember, and create order in a complex world. When dealing with men and the journey of discovering what makes you a man, I want to first talk about the alpha male label.

If you were to go into a room filled with men and ask how many identify themselves as alpha males, I am almost certain more than half the room will raise their hand. This comes from the belief that the ultimate sign of a man is the alpha male because of what comes with being labeled an alpha male. It's this belief that they are the most successful and powerful male in any group—a strong and successful man who likes to be in charge of others. The alpha male wants to dominate—who you may ask? The alpha male wants to dominate his children, his woman, and other men. He finds strength in making others feel weak.

> "Not because he went from
> baggin' up them grams to servin' O's
> Nah, your daddy was a real nigga,
> not 'cause he was hard
> Not because he lived a life of crime
> and sat behind some bars
> Not because he screamed, "Fuck the law"
> Although that was true
> Your daddy was a real nigga cause he loved you"
> **—J. Cole**

My upbringing starts off in the ghetto of Miami-Dade County. I have traveled to different cities and have been to different neighborhoods, and I've come to the realization that from coast to coast, most ghetto neighborhoods are run similarly. The players and the rules may change a bit but for the most part are about the same. The alpha male label is something that almost every man wants to cling to. In the hood it's not referred to as the alpha male. In street terms it can be referred to as a "real nigga." Most men in the hood want to be labeled an alpha male; they want to be seen as tough; they want to be "a real one." This could be the result of glamorized rap songs, gangster movies, and folklore stories or this could be the result of many falling victim to trying to identify with a label that's not suitable for them to understand the world around them better. For example, I know that a woman and children are not something you dominate. If I want a healthy relationship with anyone, be it women, children, or other men, it has to be a team effort. Seeking to dominate my teammate is not the same as seeking to dominate my opponent.

"The ignorance that make a nigga take his brother life. The bitterness and pain that got him beating on his wife." **—J. Cole**

I grew up wanting to live out the alpha male status which led to me fighting for control over others. Growing up in the environment that I grew up in led to me slowly self-destructing. When I was growing up, you had the term called OGs which stands for Original Gangster. OGs were the ones that were supposed to teach you how to execute the alpha male label. I have come to understand that most of these men were predatorial; they were looking for a young foolish guy like me that would get lost in the fake power that came with the alpha male label and carry out dominating behaviors on their behalf. They themselves were under the alpha male spell, where they were seeking to dominate the younger guys mentally, and the younger guys were carrying out the dominating acts physically. What's ironic to me is that when they are in jail, although they are dominated by a structure that tells them when to eat, when to sleep, when to shower, etc., the whole time while they are incarcerated, they fight to dominate each other. They outnumber the guards and could easily control the situation if they worked together, but due to the dominating structure, the alpha male label is only displayed amongst themselves, and it never crosses their mind to work together.

Friday Movie Scene

The main character Craig is in some trouble, and he goes to grab a gun to protect himself. His father sees him with the gun and he asks him if he feels like a man with that gun, and Craig responds, "I am a man without it."

What does that mean? That he's a man without it? Why did the father ask, "Do you feel like a man with a gun in your hand?"

You would think the OGs would offer game and give tips/tools to the younger generation, but instead they want to dominate a space they feel they have control over. To me, that's just not upright or honorable. That's not what a man is to me. For example, that alpha male label so many young men are looking to obtain, to get validation that they are a man, says that you're not tough if you exhibit emotion. To me, being tough means to possess or exhibit mental, emotional, or physical strength and resilience in challenging or difficult situations. It involves being strong-willed, determined, and having the ability to persevere and stay focused, despite obstacles or adversity. Being tough may also imply being unyielding and able to withstand hardship without giving up or becoming discouraged. It often involves having a courageous and confident attitude and the capacity to handle stress, criticism, or failure while remaining steadfast and pushing through difficult circumstances.

There can be various reasons why men may pretend to be tough. Here are a few possible explanations:

1. Societal Expectations: In many cultures, there is a traditional notion that men should be strong, stoic, and unemotional. Men may feel societal pressure to conform to this ideal of toughness, even if it means suppressing their true emotions or vulnerabilities.
2. Self-Preservation: Men may pretend to be tough as a defense mechanism to protect themselves from potential threats or harm. By projecting an image of strength, they believe they can deter others from targeting or exploiting them.
3. Peer Influence: Male relationships often involve a certain level of competitiveness and social hierar-

chy. Men may pretend to be tough to gain acceptance, fit in, or be seen as dominant within their peer group. It can be a way to maintain their status and avoid being seen as weak or inferior.

4. Emotional Masking: Some men may have grown up in environments where expressing vulnerability or sensitivity was discouraged or even ridiculed. To avoid being judged or rejected, they learn to hide their true emotions behind a tough façade.

5. Fear of Rejection: Men may fear that displaying emotions or admitting weaknesses could make them less desirable to potential romantic partners or friends. They may believe that appearing tough and self-assured makes them more attractive or desirable.

6. Cultural Conditioning: Media, movies, and popular culture often portray tough and rugged men as heroic or admirable figures. Men may be influenced by these portrayals, believing that being tough is an essential characteristic for gaining respect and admiration.

It is crucial to note that not all men pretend to be tough, and these reasons may not be applicable to every individual. People exhibit varied behaviors and characteristics, and it is important to avoid generalizations or stereotypes when discussing gender-specific behaviors.

It is important to recognize that promoting healthy and positive forms of masculinity should involve focusing on empathy, emotional well-being, equality, and respectful relationships, rather than categorizing individuals within rigid hierarchies or labels.

With what has been shared, has anything changed with your viewpoint?

WHO IS A WOMAN?

"The beauty of a woman must be seen from in her eyes, because that is the doorway to her heart, the place where love resides."
—Audrey Hepburn

When discussing who or what is a woman, we must first discuss all of the obstacles plaguing women. I believe once you see everything a woman has had to overcome this will then allow the ability to empathize and connect with what a woman is. I have a strong belief that God is more feminine than we have been made to believe. I believe that the nature of a woman not only carries life but pushes life forward. The woman has endured so much and continues to endure much, but our survival would not be possible without a woman. She is the sacred, holy place of divine creation; her fertile womb is the material wealth of all creation. The seven stages of creation are all created there, she is a fountain of supreme knowledge, wisdom, and intelligence.

The Bible is indeed one of the most influential books in history, shaping the beliefs, values, and cultures of millions of people worldwide. However, it is true that women are often portrayed in a limited or subordinate role throughout the biblical narratives. You can start with Eve eating the fruit, and she is to blame for women suffering through the end of time. Through different characters throughout the Bible such as Jezebel, Zuleikha, Bathsheba, Lot's daughters and Delilah. With this negative imprint of women, do you not see how this could raise nations that devalue what a woman is or truly appreciate their contribution to the world?

Do you know who these women are? Have you thought about how this could negatively impact women today?

The Iroquois Confederacy was under women Indian chiefs' leadership—why do I bring this up? They are responsible for the so-called founding "fathers;" they are the ones that laid down the foundation for the United States constitution as we know it today, but only men get recognized for this achievement. The mainstream recognition often overlooks the contributions of women, not only in relation to the Iroquois Confederacy, but also in general. Recognizing and highlighting their contributions is crucial for a more accurate understanding of history.

Societies often have gender roles and expectations that differentiate women's roles from men's roles. These roles can include stereotypes such as being caregivers, nurturing, or being domestic. Women often face discrimination and inequality in various aspects of life, including employment, education, political representation, and legal rights. Women may also experience gender-based violence and harassment. Women may face societal pressure to conform to certain beauty standards and expectations. This can lead to body image issues, self-esteem concerns, and sometimes unhealthy behaviors. Women often deal with reproductive rights and health-related issues, such as access to contraception, safe abortions, maternal healthcare, and addressing gender-specific health concerns.

Women had to fight for the right to go to school, the right to vote, the right to be outside at night. These are human rights that were denied to the man's counterpart. While all this was going on, what was man's role in all of this?

The Wife Beater Era

The term "wife beater era" refers to a period in history when domestic violence against women was prevalent and socially accepted to some extent. It is important to note that this term is considered derogatory, as it perpetuates negative stereotypes and makes light of a serious issue.

During this era, which can be traced back to the early 20th century, domestic violence was often overlooked or ignored by society, and victims were left without support or legal protection. The term "wife beater" itself originated from a stereotype that portrayed an abusive husband as someone who would physically assault his wife while wearing an undershirt, commonly known as a "wife beater," due to its association with this harmful behavior. In the past, women were often seen as property, with limited legal rights and societal freedom. This power dynamic led to an environment where women faced significant barriers when attempting to escape abusive relationships. Furthermore, law enforcement and legal systems often did not prioritize domestic violence cases, contributing to the acceptance and perpetuation of such abusive behavior.

After facing such afflictions, how do you think the woman would respond?

"To not protect the woman is to not protect the man and vice versa. The man is losing his humanity as long as he denies the woman hers."
—Henry J.

Thankfully, attitudes towards domestic violence have evolved significantly over time. Global movements advocating for women's rights, along with increased awareness and social consciousness, have contributed to changing societal norms and pushing for legal protection for victims of domestic violence. Organizations and initiatives now work to educate, support, and empower survivors of abuse while implementing laws to hold perpetrators accountable for their actions.

The conversation I am trying to have here is that I believe to start to heal, since life starts with a woman, we must first aid the woman—build her up and equip her to return to her natural state, not the current conditions that the world has forced her to become; once she's healthy and full of understanding, she may aid her counterpart and build him up.

There are numerous factors that make it hard for women in society. These include:

1. Gender Bias and Stereotypes: Women often face biases and stereotypes that restrict their opportunities and enforce specific roles and expectations. This includes the assumption that women are more emotional, less competent, or primarily suited for homemaking and child-rearing rather than pursuing careers or leadership positions.

2. Gender Pay Gap: Women generally earn less than men for doing the same job or work of equal value. This pay gap exists across various industries and occupations, reflecting deep-rooted gender inequalities.

3. Lack of Representation and Leadership Positions: Women are underrepresented in politics, corporate leadership positions, and decision-making roles. This limits their influence and ability to shape

policies and decisions that affect their lives and well-being.

4. Unequal Education Opportunities: In some parts of the world, women face barriers to accessing quality education. They may encounter discrimination, limited access to schools or universities, cultural norms that prioritize boys' education over girls', or negative social attitudes towards women's education and empowerment.

5. Gender-based Violence: Women are disproportionately affected by various forms of gender-based violence, including domestic violence, sexual assault, harassment, and trafficking. This not only harms their physical and mental health but also inhibits their ability to participate fully in society.

6. Lack of Maternity Support: Women often face challenges in balancing work and family responsibilities. Limited access to affordable childcare, maternity leave policies that are insufficient or nonexistent, and societal expectations regarding women's primary caregiving role make it difficult for women to advance in their careers or pursue their goals.

7. Cultural and Traditional Norms: In many societies, cultural and traditional norms perpetuate gender inequalities. These norms can restrict women's freedom, limit their choices, and enforce patriarchal power structures that prioritize men's dominance.

8. Political Underrepresentation: Women are often underrepresented in political decision-making bodies, including parliaments and other governing bodies. This leads to policies that may not adequately address women's needs and interests.

9. Objectification and Sexualization: Women are often objectified and their worth reduced to their physical appearance in media, advertising, and popular culture. This perpetuates harmful beauty standards, undermines women's agency, and reinforces gender inequality.

10. Everyday Sexism: Women often experience subtle forms of sexism and discrimination in their daily lives, including catcalling, dismissive attitudes, and double standards. These experiences can undermine women's confidence and limit their opportunities.

PARTNERSHIP

"Darling, you
You give, but you cannot take love."
—Jhené Aiko

There are many psychological and societal factors that can explain why some men struggle to receive love, despite being capable of giving love. It is important to note that these factors do not apply to all men, and individuals can have unique experiences and challenges based on their circumstances, personality traits, and upbringing. Overcoming these difficulties often involves challenging societal expectations, being aware of personal biases and conditioning, and actively working on improving emotional intelligence and communication skills. Therapy, self-reflection, and supportive relationships can also play crucial roles in helping individuals learn to receive love and emotional support.

If you got it all figured out, this is not for you.

I am hoping to share information with the ones that have been affected and are looking for a different perspective. I believe a true man is an awakened, upright individual. We are like the walking dead. When we choose to not deal with issues by getting deep and understanding the inner conflicts we have with ourselves, going to the root to understand why we respond the way that we do to the world around us, we hinder ourselves and those around us. Ask yourself, am I man enough to admit the truth of facts? Seek understanding, then to be understood. Having this lack of knowledge prevents a man from being effective and righteous. A true man understands his need for a woman.

"You know what makes me unhappy?
When brothas make babies
And leave a young mother to be a pappy
And since we all came from a woman
Got our name from a woman
and our game from a woman
I wonder why we take from our women
Why we rape our women
Do we hate our women?
I think it's time to kill for our women
Time to heal our women
be real to our women
And if we don't, we'll have a race of babies
That will hate the ladies
that make the babies

And since a man can't make one
He has no right to tell a woman
when and where to create one
So will the real men get up?"
—Tupac

A true woman is heaven; she's not a slut or a hoe. Her divine strength does not allow her to compromise to any foolishness. When you see any characteristics of a morally less, cheap, sex-starved girl, she is just that: a girl that is not a woman. That is a mentally dead girl who is a victim of this world.

Together, we will create a sanctuary where trust, love, and understanding reign. Women will acknowledge the burdens men bear and assure them that solace can be found within our safe space. We will provide unwavering support and work side by side to achieve common goals. Men will recognize the societal pressures that have devalued women and vow to treat them as equals. They will acknowledge that their own worth is intertwined with the women in their lives, understanding that neglecting or rejecting them is ultimately self-destructive.

In this safe space, we will foster an environment free from judgment and prejudice. We will embrace one another's differences and celebrate our unique contributions. Together, we will build a haven where every individual feels valued, heard, seen, and loved.

THE SPIRITUAL BODY

Is the religion you practice spiritual or ritual?
What does it mean to be spiritual?

Our personal emotions, though valid and important, can sometimes cloud our judgment and prevent us from accepting the truth. It takes courage to set aside our ego and biases and embrace the uncomfortable reality that the truth brings. Moreover, seeking the truth requires a certain level of detachment from our personal emotions. Emotions can be heightened, subjective, and biased, which could lead us astray from objective facts. By acknowledging this and striving to approach the truth with an open mind, we can overcome these personal barriers and gain a deeper understanding of the world.

The truth may not always be pleasant or comforting. It may challenge our beliefs, expose our mistakes, or force us to confront uncomfortable realities. However, it is only by embracing the truth that we can remove the blinders from our eyes and the barriers from our hearts. It is through knowing the truth that we can truly grow and evolve as individuals and as a society.

Let us not allow our personal emotions to hinder our pursuit of truth. Let us be brave enough to confront the discomfort it may bring and open ourselves to the possibilities of growth and understanding. Only then can we become more enlightened, compassionate, and empathetic beings.

When I was younger, I would always have questions about religion but was discouraged about asking them. I was told never to question God; God gave us inquisitive brains so that we could question and learn, but those who are ignorant of the true knowledge of God will discourage you from questioning them because they are fearful of their own ignorance, which shows their inability to legitimately answer your legitimate questions.

In other words, they don't know what they are talking about, so they are scared to answer questions due to ego and pride.

We must always seek and ask questions or we will stop growing in our knowledge. You can't receive any answers of understanding unless you first ask questions of non-understanding. I just don't have this belief or understanding that God would be upset or against you for seeking Him and wanting to understand Him. There are a lot of religious people in the world but not a lot of spiritual people. You must understand this: to be religious doesn't mean spiritual.

There are a lot of people who are religious in practice, but they are not spiritual in their nature.

A religion doesn't automatically make you a spiritual person; a religion just provides you with the blueprint.

To be religious is to habitually practice rituals of a particular religion. I am not here to debate if a religious ritual is good or bad, just pointing out that, in fact, these religious practices are rituals. A ritual doesn't have to be viewed as a negative unless it's used negatively. A particular religious organization's rituals are centered around certain ideas and doctrine. A religious organization of religious ritual aims at attaining spirituality.

We have different religions,
but I believe that there is but one **GOD**.
We have all these different religions,
but they all have the same goal: spirituality.

If we have one goal and one God,
then what are we fighting for?

The path to spirituality is not through division. True spirituality comes from within, through personal self-reflection and a deep connection with the divine. It is not tied to any religious title or name. Unfortunately, some individuals who claim to represent God use their positions to spread hate, prejudice, and intolerance. They create barriers between people of different religions and communities, rather than promoting unity and compassion.

It is essential to recognize these imposters for what they are and not let their actions tarnish the true essence of religion. We must strive to follow the teachings of our faiths that promote love, kindness, and respect for all human beings, regardless of their religious backgrounds. Let us work toward building bridges of understanding and cooperation between different religions and communities, rather than erecting walls of division. Let us strive to be true spiritual beings who embody the values of compassion, forgiveness, and unity.

ENERGY

The body creates energy through the chemical energy process.

In this place of pure energy, we tap into the infinite potential that resides within us. It is the realm where all ideas, thoughts, and possibilities originate. When we open ourselves up to this realm, we transcend the limitations of our conditioned beliefs and expand our perception of what is possible. To access this power, we must create a fertile environment within ourselves. This begins by quieting the mind and letting go of the constant chatter and noise that often dominates our thoughts. Through meditation, mindfulness, or other practices, we create space for a deeper connection with our higher brain.

The higher brain, also known as the intuitive mind or the higher self, holds the key to unlocking our true potential. It is the part of us that is connected to the universal consciousness, where all knowledge and wisdom reside. By tuning into this aspect of ourselves, we can tap into profound insights, inner peace, and boundless creativity. The experience of enlightenment arises when we fully awaken to the power of our higher brain. It is a state of expanded consciousness where we no longer identify solely with our ego or limited beliefs. Instead, we become aware of our interconnectedness with all of existence, experiencing a profound sense of unity and love.

In this state, we can perceive the world from a place of deep understanding and compassion. We are guided by intuition and inner wisdom, making decisions that align with our higher purpose and the greater good. Our creativity flows effortlessly as we tap into the infinite possibilities that exist within the realm of pure energy. Enlightenment is not a destination but rather an ongoing journey of self-discovery and growth. It requires a willingness to let go of old patterns and beliefs that no longer serve us, and to continuously expand our awareness and understanding.

As we embrace the power of the higher brain and cultivate a fertile environment for its expression, we awaken to the limitless potential that resides within us. We tap into the wellspring of pure energy that fuels our transformation and empowers us to create a life of fulfillment, joy, and purpose.

The problem is in our hearts;
our hearts need to be transformed

You may go to church but perhaps you are still searching. There is an empty place in your heart, and something inside tells you that you're not right with God. Nicodemus fasted two days a week. He spent two hours every day in prayer. He tithed, but he was told he must be born again.

Why did Jesus say that Nicodemus must be born again?

To do anything we need an energy source. The body creates energy through the process of a chemical reaction. This is because of the reaction of atoms. All the elements we take into our bodies—oxygen, potassium, calcium, and sodium—have specific charges. When we eat or drink, the molecules break down in our body and work; this process is called cellular respiration. All the things we take into our bodies allow us to have electrical impulses. Electricity is required for the nervous system to send signals throughout the body and to the brain, making it possible for us to move, think, and feel.

If we have this understanding that our body is an energy source, how do you protect your energy?

How do you make sure that your energy exchange is positive?

VIBRATION

"If we accept that sound is vibration and we know that vibration touches every part of our physical being, then we understand that sound is heard not only through our ears but through every cell in our bodies." **—Integrative Oncologist Dr. Mitchell Gaynor**

Vibrational sound therapy can retune your body, mind, and spirit, encouraging relaxation, healing, and wellness.

When you engage in relaxation techniques that involve soothing sounds and vibrations, the effects can reach down to a cellular level within your body. This process helps to restore and enhance the flow of energy, bringing you back toward a state of healthy alignment. Stress, on the other hand, disrupts the natural flow of energy within your body. Initially, it may manifest as a low energy state within your aura, a subtle energetic field that surrounds and interpenetrates your physical body. Over time, if left unaddressed, this disrupted energy flow can contribute to the development of mental and physical illnesses.

> Have you ever heard the phrases
> 'good vibes' and 'bad vibes'?

When our bodies and minds are vibrating at a healthy level, we generally feel well inside and out. When we encounter negative or draining environments or people, our vibrational frequency can be lowered, making us more susceptible to illness and mood issues. However, by utilizing the vibrations and frequencies produced by sound, you can help restore balance and improve overall well-being. For example, clapping hands or strumming a guitar creates vibrations that are transmitted through the air and converted into soundwaves, which the brain interprets as sound.

> Vibration really is a keyword.

Sound energy has been used for centuries in various spiritual practices and rituals. It is believed to have the ability to cleanse and purify the soul, allowing for spiritual growth and transformation. Chanting mantras, singing hymns, or practicing sound therapy are some ways in which sound energy is used to tap into the spiritual realm.

Furthermore, sound energy is closely linked to emotions. Certain sounds, such as soothing music or nature sounds, have a calming effect on the mind and can help relieve stress and anxiety. On the other hand, loud, jarring noises can trigger feelings of unease or even anger. This showcases the profound impact sound has on our emotional well-being.

In addition to its effect on the mind and emotions, sound energy also has the potential to heal the body. Sound therapy, also known as sound healing, utilizes vibrations and frequencies to restore balance and harmony within the body. It is believed that certain sounds can stimulate the body's natural healing processes and aid in physical recovery.

The power of sound extends beyond our individual experiences. It is a universal language that transcends cultural and language barriers. Music, for example, has the ability to bring people from different backgrounds together, evoking shared emotions and creating a sense of unity and connection.

However, the power of sound can also be wielded in negative ways. Harsh words, insults, and hateful language have the capacity to hurt and wound others deeply. It is important to be mindful of the words we use and the energy that our speech carries. By choosing to communicate with kindness and compassion, we can create a positive and harmonious environment for ourselves and those around us. Sound energy is a potent force that is intricately connected to our consciousness and spirituality. It has the power to influence our emotions, heal our bodies, and connect us with others. We must recognize and respect its immense power, using it wisely and with intention.

HUMANITY

There's no hotline to dial to say the world needs help.

Before the civil war, psychiatrists diagnosed slaves with what they called drapetomania: a mental illness in which the slave possessed an irrational desire for freedom and tendency to try to escape.

Could you believe that someone once said you have a mental illness because you have a desire to want human rights and the freedom to exist?

Some "experts" diagnosed slaves with a mental illness simply because they yearned for freedom and attempted to escape their oppressive conditions. This misguided perspective reflects the deeply ingrained prejudice and injustice prevalent during that time period.

This Black and White Thing

I find no pleasure in doing this, and I am aware that it is inappropriate and unproductive to diagnose or label an entire racial group, including white people, based on a specific historical context. I am also aware that when you put something like this under a microscope you should examine the socio-cultural, economic, and political factors that influenced the behaviors, attitudes, and beliefs of people during that time period. But for the sake of addressing this black and white issue, I think it will help me paint the picture that I want to paint. We just discussed how they came out with a mental illness describing black slaves during that time. I thought I would diagnose the white people during that time to highlight how irresponsible and insensitive this can be.

The diagnosis: *Antisocial personality disorder*

This is a mental health condition characterized by a pervasive pattern of disregard for and violation of the rights of others. Those with this condition often engage in manipulative, deceitful, and irresponsible behavior without feeling remorse or empathy for the harm they cause to others.

They have difficulty understanding and relating to the feelings and experiences of others. They may disregard the needs, feelings, and rights of others, leading to a disregard for societal norms. People with this disorder often act impulsively without considering the consequences of their actions. They may engage in criminal activities. They may lie, manipulate, or exploit others for personal gain without feeling guilty or remorseful. They may engage in aggressive behaviors, such as bullying, physical fights. They have little to no remorse or guilt for the harm they cause to others. They may rationalize their behavior or blame others to avoid taking responsibility for their actions.

Let's look at the programming of all the slave books, movies, and documentaries the government, schools, and media have shown you over your lifetime. Wouldn't the white people they depreciate during these times fit the mental illness? You want to know what's the worst part about all of this? Through time this behavior, this psychosis, has never been addressed because people are afraid to say the hard things, to look in the mirror, and call it like it is!

It runs deep—they do not trust *white* people.

It is important to recognize that generalizations about any racial or ethnic group are not accurate or fair. It is not accurate to say that all black people hate white people, just as it is not accurate to claim that all white people harbor negative attitudes toward black people. Individuals' beliefs and attitudes are shaped by a multitude of factors, including personal experiences, upbringing, and social influences. However, like any other diverse group, including white people, there may be individuals within the black community who hold negative or prejudiced views toward people of other races, including the white community. It is essential to understand that these individuals do not represent the beliefs of all black people.

For a moment, I will play devil's advocate, I want to examine this idea that *Black* people hate *white* people, and when I say this, I want you to ask the question: Could you blame them for hating *white* people? I mean, can you truly disagree that a *black* person hating a *white* person is a bad thing? I think the opposite: I find it foolish for a *black* person to not hate a *white* person. I am a God-fearing man, and I know you have been taught that you should not hate, so I want to remove myself and ideas. I want to hate what God hates, and you know what I have come to find out?

Below are God's instructions. If you are to follow his ways, to be a reflection of Him, you should hate these things as well:

- Proverbs 16:5
  - » Prideful person

- Proverbs 6:16–19
  - » a lying tongue
  - » hands that shed innocent blood
  - » a heart that devises wicked schemes
  - » feet that are quick to rush into evil
  - » a false witness who pours out lies
  - » a person who stirs up conflict in the community

So as a *black* person going through slavery knowing what God hates, how could it be that you not hate a *white* person? (I am not saying to hate anyone, simply asking to digest this train of thought.)It's like someone putting their foot on your neck, choking you out, and you in turn say I cannot hate this person because…

"If a black man has to be responsible for every day of his life for something that he did not do, that he has to pay for the history, for the color of his skin, white people must pay as well. The great pain is that you cannot get across to the white person that you as human as he is."
—James Baldwin

We had a time period where there were laws that:
- banned against a slave owning a weapon.
- banned a black person from testifying against a white person in court.
- prevented blacks from owning drums or horn instruments.
- prohibited blacks from taking part in any kind of trade.
- in New York, three or more black people were refused meeting up at once.

And if we are being honest, it's still going on today, just in different forms.

Even when you converted into a Christian, that conversion would not change your slave status. Law enforcement was given the authority to search and whip slaves if they appear to have disorderly behavior.

There are more black males than females born in the United States; however, by the time the two reach eighteen, when factoring in incarceration, homicide, suicide, black females outnumber black males seven to one. The black males are effectively dying at the rate of endangered species.

Now I know at this time I might have triggered a few people or made them feel uncomfortable, but when I am throwing out shades of color, black/white, I want you to think: why are you uncomfortable?

I know the answer is because you identify with one of these groups. Whether black or white. One side being black saying, "I am black, and I don't want to hate anyone." The other side being white and you are saying, "I do not want to be hated." I want to say both of you are right; however, you're looking at things in the wrong way. You separated yourself black and white off of the color or your skin. You fell right into the trap to think that you are different because your paint jobs are different. It is not as if blacks are from Mars and whites are from Pluto. All humans, regardless of race, religion, or background, share a common origin. It is essential to recognize and appreciate our shared humanity.

It is also important to acknowledge the historical and social factors that have led to the division and discrimination we see today. Throughout history, humans have constructed systems of power and privilege that have marginalized certain groups, based on characteristics such as race, ethnicity, and religion. Understanding and confronting these systems of inequality must be an ongoing process. It requires education, empathy, open-mindedness, and a willingness to challenge our own biases and prejudices. It is crucial to listen to the experiences and perspectives of others and work towards creating a more just and inclusive society for everyone. By promoting understanding and embracing diversity, we can strive to dismantle the barriers that separate us and build a world where everyone is valued and respected.

COLOR GAMES

Cry Freedom movie, court scene:
Why do you call yourself black?
You look more brown than black.

Steve Biko: *Why do you call yourselves white?*
You look more pink than white.

Those in power have been using various tactics to keep people divided and hurt throughout history. Here are some common tricks they have employed:

1. Divide and conquer: This strategy involves creating divisions and animosities among different groups within society, such as along ethnic, religious, or socioeconomic lines. By pitting these groups against each other, those in power can distract people from their shared grievances and maintain control.

2. Propaganda and disinformation: Manipulating information and spreading propaganda is a sig-

nificant tool for those in power to control public opinion. They can disseminate false narratives that demonize and dehumanize specific groups, leading to heightened tensions and further division.

3. Creating scapegoats: By targeting certain individuals or groups as the cause of societal problems, those in power can divert attention from their own failures and injustices. Blaming a particular group for issues such as economic inequality or political instability creates division and fosters resentment toward the scapegoated group.

4. Suppressing dissent: Those in power often employ tactics to silence and marginalize critics and opposition. By limiting freedom of speech, assembly, or the press, they can control the dissemination of alternative perspectives and discourage collective action against their rule.

5. Exploiting identity politics: Manipulating identity-based issues and using them as political tools can polarize communities and pit different groups against each other. By stoking fear, anger, or resentment around identity markers such as race, religion, or gender, those in power can maintain divisive power dynamics.

6. Promoting economic inequality: A society with significant income and wealth disparities inherently perpetuates divisions. By favoring policies that concentrate wealth and power in the hands of a few,

those in power can create environments of social unrest and perpetuate divisions between the privileged and the marginalized.

There is in fact but one race, of many colors.

HOW WE GOT DIVIDED

no church in the wild

The titles Black American and African American are fake, inappropriate European titles, created to keep indigenous people (aka Indian) of the western hemisphere (the Americas) under a spell of ignorance. "Black American" and "African American" implies that African Americans are only connected to America and Africa, but they are not African nor have any connection to Africa, and they are accepted in America only as second class. They have been stripped of their true indigenous identity. This can lead to a psychological and spiritual disconnect because they cannot connect to their heritage. For example, Jesse Jackson, a South Carolina Cherokee Indian, started to promote the fake title of African American that has been imposed upon black Indians, indigenous to the western hemisphere.

What law did Virginia pass in 1705?
What was the Virginia weapons law in 1723?

In 1705, Virginia passed the Virginia Slave Code, also known as "An Act Concerning Servants and Slaves." This law defined the legal status and treatment of enslaved black Indians and their descendants, establishing a system of chattel slavery in the colony. It restricted the rights and freedoms of enslaved people, denying them basic human rights, and ensuring their owners had complete control over their lives and labor. The Virginia Slave Code set a precedent for future slave laws in other colonies and states.

European powers sought to establish dominance and exploit resources in other parts of the world. This often involved the subjugation and control of indigenous populations. In order to justify this domination, Europeans developed ideologies of racial superiority which considered people of European descent as superior to those of other races. During this period Europeans (Whites) were given guns and food and rights to vote, while others were stripped of their rights.

The reason for this was because together the Europeans (Whites) and the Indians (Blacks) outnumbered the people in charge of power structure. After the Bacon rebellion, the Europeans were not given the ability to move up in class, so the idea was to give them something else, and what they gave them was power over another group of people; so they sold them the idea of a "white identity." This was done to reinforce the belief in the inherent superiority of Europeans. By creating a concept of whiteness, Europeans attempted to create a sense of unity and social cohesion among themselves, while excluding people of color from the same privileges and rights.

This system of racial hierarchy created significant disparities in power, wealth, and social status. It entrenched prejudices and discrimination, leading to the marginalization and oppression of non-white populations. Over time, these racial divisions have had far-reaching consequences, having shaped social, economic, and political structures in numerous societies.

Did you know before the Bacon rebellion, the term white or black to describe a person was not ever used? Do you now see the impact that this had on how we live today?

EDUCATION

Once your kids start school they will be in school more than they are at home.

The industrial age was good for America/bad for American people.

We made a switch as a society from hunter-gatherers to agricultural and then to the industrial age and now in technology. The earliest human beings didn't need schools to pass along information. They educated youngsters on an individual basis within the family unit. Over time, however, populations grew, and societies formed. Rather than every family being individually responsible for education, people soon figured out that it would be easier and more efficient to have a small group of adults teach a larger group of children. In this way, the concept of the school was born. Ancient schools weren't like the schools we know today, though. The earliest schools often focused more on teaching skills and passing along religious values, rather than teaching specific subject areas as is common today.

In the United States, the first school was the Boston Latin School, which was founded in 1635. It was the first public school and the oldest existing school in the country. The earliest schools focused on reading, writing, and mathematics. The New England colonies led the way in requiring towns to set up schools. The Massachusetts Bay Colony made basic education a requirement in 1642. However, many of the earliest schools were only for boys, and there were usually few, if any, options for girls.

In 1833, the government passed the Factory Act, making two hours of education a day compulsory for children working in factories. The government also granted money to charities for schools for the first time. The moment that money began to influence the education system it led us down the wrong path. One could assume the decision to grant money to charities for schools was likely a response to the growing concern for improving access to education for the working class. By providing financial support to charities, the government aimed to expand educational opportunities and bridge the gap between the privileged and underprivileged. However, introducing money into the education system created risks. The influence of money and the potential for corruption led to the prioritization of profit over quality education. This resulted in ill-equipped teachers, inadequate resources, and a focus on monetary gains rather than the holistic development of students.

During the industrial age, the school was designed to get people equipped and prepared for the workforce, which was mostly factory work during that time. The designs of the classroom were set up like an assembly line because it was supposed to prepare the students for their jobs in the factories. Unfortunately, we are still following this model even though times have changed. The school system has not. The habits we pick up in school no longer create economic value. In fact, we may be learning to destroy value. There is a saying that knowledge is power, but there is little to no value in education in America. Many students take an entitlement stance because it is offered for "free." The concepts of what it costs to run a school are lost because students are so frustrated with the school environment; they don't even have room to care. That's the biggest obstacle; they lost the desire to be in school.

The credit for our modern version of the school system usually goes to Horace Mann. When he became Secretary of Education in Massachusetts in 1837, he set forth his vision for a system of professional teachers who would teach students an organized curriculum of basic content. By 1918, every state required students to complete elementary school. Educational improvements grew by leaps and bounds during the 20th century, leading to the advanced systems we have today. After the American Revolution, education became a higher priority. States quickly began to establish public schools. School systems were not uniform, however, and would often vary greatly from state to state.

The two major ideas that should be taught to children of every country are:

1. The value of the individual
2. The fact of one humanity

There are three duties of education:
- The first effort for education to civilize the child is to train and rightly direct his instincts.
- The second obligation is to be able to bring about the child's true culture (not the history of who won the war), training him to use his intellect rightly.
- The third duty of education is to bring out and to develop intuition.

When these three are developed and functioning, you will have a civilized, cultured, and spiritually awakened human being; a person will then be instinctively correct and intellectually sound and intuitively aware. Their souls, their minds, and their brains will be functioning as the should and in right relation to each other, thus again producing coordination and correct alignment.

1. An atmosphere of love: Where fear is cast out and the child realizes he has no cause of shyness or caution. The child receives respectful treatment from others and is expected to also give respectful treatment to others in return. Love always draws forth what is best in a child.
2. An atmosphere of patience: The child can become normally and naturally a seeker after knowledge; the child is always met with a careful response to

questions, and there is not a sense of speed or hurry (opposite of what happens when trying to prepare a student for a standardized test).

3. An atmosphere of ordered activity: Where the child can learn the first principles of responsibility. When the child is developing a sense of responsibility, it will factor in determining a child's character and future career.

4. An atmosphere of understanding: Where a child is always sure of the reason and motives for his actions, although we may not always approve of what the child has done. It is always the older generation that fosters in a child an early and unnecessary guilt of wrongdoing. Much importance is laid upon petty things that are not really wrong, but annoying to parents or teachers. The true sense is not recognized for what it is, failure to understand the child. If these aspects of the child's life are handled right, then true wrong things, the violation of others, the hurting and damaging others in order to achieve personal gain, will emerge in the right attitude and at the right time.

A better education system should prioritize teaching empathy and understanding to students. By incorporating empathy training into the curriculum, students can learn to put themselves in others' shoes, understand different perspectives, and appreciate diversity. This will help break down barriers and reduce prejudices by promoting a more compassionate and inclusive society. The curriculum should include lessons that challenge and debunk stereotypes and prejudices. Education should provide accurate and balanced information about different cultures, races, religions, genders, and socioeconomic backgrounds. By addressing biases and misconceptions head-on, students can develop a more open-minded and accepting mindset. The education system should promote collaboration, teamwork, and communication skills. These skills are crucial for fostering understanding and building harmonious relationships with others.

By incorporating these values into the curriculum, promoting cultural exchanges, and developing teachers' cultural competence, we can break down barriers, remove prejudices, and raise a new generation capable of living in harmony and goodwill with others.

WHAT DID YOU SAY?

We once all spoke one language; a time when we were connected with the world around us. During this era, communication flowed effortlessly between individuals, tribes, and cultures, transcending boundaries, and fostering unity. People shared stories, knowledge, and experiences, enabling them to understand and empathize with one another. This common language served as a powerful tool for cooperation and collaboration in the pursuit of collective goals. People could work together seamlessly, harnessing their combined strengths and talents to build prosperous communities and advance their societies. The world was a vibrant tapestry of diverse cultures, all interconnected through this shared language.

The benefits of this shared language extended beyond interpersonal communication. It facilitated the exchange of ideas, innovations, and scientific advancements. With a common language, discoveries made in one part of the world could be shared and built upon by others, sparking a rapid acceleration of progress and development. Moreover, this shared language fostered a deep connection to the natural world. People understood their interconnectedness with nature, recognizing the importance of stewardship and living in harmony with the environment. This wisdom was passed down through generations, ensuring the preservation of ecosystems and biodiversity.

However, as time went on, the unity and interconnectedness began to erode. The proliferation of different languages and the resulting linguistic barriers led to misunderstandings and divisions. Cultural differences became increasingly highlighted and emphasized, creating a sense of "us versus them" mentality. Today, we exist in a world fragmented by numerous languages, each with its unique cultural nuances and barriers. This linguistic diversity enriches our global tapestry, but it also presents challenges in communication and understanding.

Nonetheless, the remnants of that once-shared language can still be observed in certain universal aspects of human expression, like music, art, and emotions. These bridges offer glimpses of our shared humanity, reminding us that despite our linguistic differences, we are all interconnected and part of a larger global family. As we navigate this evolving world, it is crucial to remember the power of language as a means of connection and understanding.

Why does this matter? How does this impact how students learn today?

Do you understand how insensitive it is to mock
a child coming from the inner city, speaking
"Hood English" or Spanglish? That is an attack
on their culture.

Cultural diversity and language variations are essential aspects of our society, and we should encourage understanding and appreciation rather than ridicule. Education plays
a crucial role in ensuring effective communication skills. It
is important to teach children the appropriate context and
register for different situations, including when to use more
formal or standardized English. However, it is equally important to respect and acknowledge the various forms of
language and dialects spoken within different communities.
Promoting inclusivity, providing support, and encouraging
language development without belittling or attacking any
cultural background should be the goal.

Love

Love must be practical, tested manifestation, and not just
theory or just an idea and a pleasing sentiment. It is something that has grown in the trials and tests of life. Love for
many people is not really love but a mixture of desire to love
and the desire to be loved, plus the willingness to do anything to show and evoke this sentiment. Love is not a sentiment or an emotion, nor is it desire or a selfish motive for
right actions in daily life. Love is a force that leads to unity

and inclusiveness; it's an action. Love is hard; it is a challenge; it's a difficult thing to apply to all conditions of life and its expression; it will demand the utmost you have to give; it removes your selfish personal tendencies/activities.

To know love is to know pain. If you search and understand the power that is in dealing with pain, you may then also open the door for you to understand love. Pain is the cold of isolation which leads to the warmth of the sun; pain is getting burned and finally knowing/appreciating the coolness of water. Pain is stepping out in the world, getting chewed up and spit out, and love is coming back into a welcoming home. Pain leads the human soul out of darkness into light, out of bondage into liberation, out of agony into peace.

Animals suffer physically and sentiently. A person suffers physically, sentiently, and also mentally. Mental suffering is due to aspects in the lower mind such as anticipation, memory, imagination, remorse, and the inherent urge to be accepted, which brings the sense of loss and failure. We seek to avoid pain, but it is the protector of substance. It warns you of danger. It is this process, related to the soul defining itself with substance, when pain, disease, and death lose their hold on a person. The soul no longer subjected to these requirements and now at this point you are free. Pain is not something you should run from; it is a purifier when address and met properly.

We talked about pain, we talked about love, and as you go through this thing called life, you will be hurt by both.

Love and pain come with hurt, so let's talk about healing. Healing comes from knowledge. When entering the
world of healing, you must come with the intention to gain
knowledge and apply it. When someone comes to the state
of truly open-mindedness and is ready to accept new information and theories, they discover the old and dearly held
truth is not lost but only regulated to its rightful place in a
larger scheme. It's like watching from a different perspective. It makes you more powerful because now you can see
things from a wide range. For example, in my background
in playing football, there is this famous saying: The eye in
the sky does not lie. A coach on the field may see something
one way, the player playing may see it in a different way,
but when you go look at it from the person recording and
getting all the angles, you gain more knowledge of the situation; you can see it better and do better. One must seek and
want to do better for themselves if they want to heal. As
discussed earlier we are spiritual beings, high energy people.

The self-will and energy that individuals release in their
quest for healing have immense power to bring about their
own healing. By nurturing the forces they desire to utilize,
they can harness the potential to transform their physical,
emotional, and spiritual well-being. To effectively channel
these healing energies, individuals must cultivate discipline
and control over their appetites. This includes not only di-
etary choices but also the thoughts and emotions they in-
dulge in. By building a clean body, free from toxins and negative influences, they create a conducive environment for

the easy flow of healing forces through their own being and to others.

By adopting a disciplined approach and creating clear channels, individuals can tap into the self-will and release energy that brings about healing on multiple levels. This involves actively engaging in practices like meditation, mindfulness, healthy eating, regular exercise, and self-reflection. Through these practices, individuals can cultivate a higher state of consciousness that facilitates the healing process.

Love prescription
In love is a temporary emotional high,
and you need to pursue real love.

Being in love gives you an illusion that you're in an intimate relationship, where you feel you belong to each other. "I would do anything to make you happy." We believe that he/she will be committed to meeting our needs, that he/she loves us as much as we love him/her, and that he/she would never do anything to hurt us. That thinking is always fanciful. We become blind to the fact that everyone has their own flaws, insecurities, and selfish tendencies. This illusion of love can lead to disappointment and heartbreak when we realize that our partner is not perfect and cannot fulfill all of our expectations. We may start to question their love for us, feeling betrayed and hurt when they act in ways that go against our idealized image of them.

It is important to recognize that love is not a fairy tale; it requires effort, compromise, and acceptance of each other's imperfections. Realizing that both individuals in a relationship are egocentric beings with their own needs and desires allows for a more realistic and grounded approach to love. Instead of expecting our partner to always put us first and never hurt us, we should strive for open communication, understanding, and mutual growth. By acknowledging our own egocentric nature and that of our partner, we can foster a healthier and more balanced relationship based on empathy, compromise, and realistic expectations.

Talk to me nice!

No one has ever hurt you; it is the way that you look at life; it comes from your programing. A person cannot understand you or be there for you if they don't understand how you see the world. I am aware of the importance that external factors and the actions of others can cause, but we are here to discuss how you take control of your life. You begin working on yourself first.

Our outlook and perceptions can shape our experiences in life. If we have a negative or distorted view of the world, it can impact how we interpret and respond to situations.

While our personal perspective plays a significant role in how we navigate life, it does not negate the possibility of others causing us pain.

He cheats & it hurts...
A wise person can play a fool,
but a fool can't play wise.

If you are able to change your conditional wiring and understand that he didn't cheat on you, he just cheats. It's the perspective or a realization that cheating is not specific to you or your relationship. It's the understanding that the actions are not a reflection of your worth or a result of something lacking in your relationship, but rather a pattern of behavior that the other person engages in regardless of the circumstances.

If it hurts, it is about you trying to fix something unfixable or unwilling to change. It's the idea that if you choose to be in a relationship with someone who has a history of cheating or does not have a moral code, that it's wrong; you should not be surprised or hurt when they continue to cheat. It is the individual's own responsibility to choose someone who aligns with their values and expectations in order to avoid pain and disappointment. Cheating reflects the cheater's character rather than a personal attack on the person they are in a relationship with. Therefore, the onus is on the individual to make these choices wisely and be aware of the consequences.

It's the emotional punishment you give yourself for someone else's behavior. That was not your issue, but you took it as your issue.

Building relationships requires time, effort, and careful consideration. It is crucial to understand the person you are getting involved with before fully committing and allowing them into your life. By doing so, you take on the responsibility of who enters your world, knowing that once someone is a part of your life, you cannot control their actions or decisions.

Learning the person you are giving yourself to involves various aspects, such as understanding their values, beliefs, and goals. It means being attentive to their behavior, observing how they treat others, and assessing their compatibility with your own principles. It requires patience and curiosity to explore their interests, past experiences, and motivations. By investing time in this process, you can gain insight into their character, integrity, and overall suitability as a partner, friend, or any other role they might play in your life.

Taking responsibility for who you allow into your world is vital, because the people we surround ourselves with have a significant impact on our well-being and personal growth. Their words, actions, and energy can influence our emotions, attitudes, and even our own behavior. Therefore, it is essential to evaluate whether someone aligns with our values and supports our personal development.

While it is impossible to control others once they are in our life, we can pave the way for healthy relationships by setting boundaries and expressing our expectations. Communicating openly and honestly about our needs, desires, and concerns can foster understanding and create a foundation of trust. However, it is important to recognize that each individual is ultimately responsible for their own thoughts, choices, and actions.

It is crucial to take your time and learn about the person you are allowing into your life. By taking on the responsibility of who enters your world, you can make more informed decisions and surround yourself with individuals who are compatible with your values, goals, and overall well-being. Remember that while you cannot control others, open communication and setting boundaries can contribute to healthy relationships.

FAMILY

The family unit serves as the foundational building block of society.

The importance of the family unit in society cannot be overstated. Family is the first source of socialization for individuals. From an early age, children learn societal norms, values, and moral principles within the family. This contributes to their overall development and helps shape their character and behavior. Family provides emotional support and acts as a safety net. Members of the family can rely on each other during times of joy, sorrow, stress, or crisis. This support system promotes mental and emotional well-being, which is crucial for individuals to flourish in society. It is a place where individuals feel safe and protected. This stability creates a sense of belonging, which promotes healthier relationships and a stronger sense of identity.

The family unit influences physical health and overall well-being. Healthy habits, such as proper nutrition, exercise, and self-care are often reinforced within the family. Additionally, family members provide emotional and caregiving support during illness or times of poor health. Families are also vital for the transmission of cultural values, traditions, and heritage. Through generations, families pass down customs, cultural practices, and important stories that connect individuals to their roots and help foster a sense of identity. Strong families contribute to the social fabric, promoting stability, resilience, and overall well-being within the larger community.

Change is inevitable.

Change is necessary for the survival and growth of any entity, including the family unit. As society evolves, so do the circumstances, challenges, and expectations faced by families. Adapting to these changes and understanding the need for transformation is vital for the family unit to thrive.

The Wire TV series

Preston 'Bodie' Broadus: "And then I'm standing here like an asshole, holding my Charles Dickens 'cause I ain't got no muscle, no backup. Shit man, yo, if this was the old days..."

Slim Charles: "Yeah now, well, the thing about the old days...they the old days."

One crucial factor driving the need for change in the family unit is the shifting dynamics of gender roles and expectations. Traditional gender roles, where men were typically the breadwinners, while women took care of the household and children, have significantly evolved. Today, families are becoming more egalitarian, with both partners sharing responsibilities and contributing to the financial well-being of the household. Embracing this change can lead to greater partnership and harmony within the family.

Relationships between men and women are suffering in a major way.

The historical struggles between men and women, where power dynamics have caused harm and oppression, have had a significant impact on the advancement of gender equality. The feminist movement sought to address these imbalances, but sometimes, when previously oppressed groups come into power, they repeat the same patterns. Sexism and racism are both forms of discrimination and prejudice, but they manifest in different ways and have distinct historical and social contexts.

This cycle creates division and dehumanization, ultimately hurting everyone involved. The key is to acknowledge past failures, understand their impact on both men and women, and work together to build a more equal and unified society. Breaking it down to my sports background, when it's playoff time and you go on a run to try to win a championship, ego has to go out the window. One game this guy may have an amazing game, and the next game, the other team works to shut him down. That's when someone else has an opportunity to have a good game. This analogy of teamwork in sports emphasizes the importance of setting aside personal egos and working collaboratively within the family unit to raise children who are prepared to challenge the harsh world they are going to have to live in.

> No one follows a fool unless they are fools
> themselves.

Although it's in man's nature to naturally be aggressive because men have a high level of testosterone, you cannot misuse your nature. Being a man does not inherently mean dominating over something or someone. Masculinity can be defined in various ways and should not be limited to aggression or dominance. Being a man can involve qualities such as empathy, compassion, and nurturing, which are equally important for personal growth and building healthy relationships. True leadership and guidance are not about forcing one's authority but rather about serving the needs of others. Effective leadership requires responsibility, knowledge, and wisdom, which can be developed through experience, education, and self-reflection.

Men can support women's rights by advocating for equal opportunities for women in all areas of life, including education, employment, and leadership positions. This includes actively listening to women's voices, supporting their ideas and initiatives, and challenging any form of discrimination or harassment. By embracing a more holistic under-standing of masculinity, men can contribute to a more equal and just society for everyone.

The world puts this oppression on women they sexual-ize and stripped down to being brainless, and thoughtless. I don't find it wise to associate with any of these negative characteristics! I want to point out that a lot of women have played into the male chauvinism as a way of sitting back and taking very little initiative to develop their own po-tential, and just want to live off a man like a leech. If you operate in that manner, your lack of motivation and inspi-ration is just as poor as the egotistical male you choose as your partner that is oppressing you. To just want someone to take you, and you are a grown adult, is counterproduc-tive. I encourage women to develop their own potential and build together with their partners, rather than relying solely on them for survival.

MONEY

If the hood is so poor, explain gentrification

Don't you find it crazy that someone could live in the hood, and because of the daily violence, the struggle, they truly believe that they are poor? At the same time, someone else comes up with a great idea and says this would be a great spot to have a spa or a coffee shop. Due to the daily exposure to violence and struggling conditions in an impoverished area, it creates a mindset where individuals believe that poverty is the only reality for them.

However, great ideas and opportunities can arise from any situation, even in areas facing difficulties. The potential for development and improvement exists in all communities, regardless of their current state. It is important to provide support, resources, and opportunities to uplift communities and empower individuals to break free from the cycle of poverty and violence.

One man's trash is another man's treasure.

This thing is all about perception. I am challenging young people to look at their community as something to be proud of. I know growing up in chaos and poverty makes it hard, and that often the goal is to "make it out" of those circumstances. However, remember that someone from outside the community sees the potential and value that you don't recognize. There are untapped opportunities and resources within your community you should appreciate and take advantage of.

American citizens have become spoiled and lazy. I believe that we have one of the highest levels of poverty. What I mean by that is when you compare a poor person in Dubai to a poor person in Liberty City or a poor person in Columbia to a poor person on the southside of Houston, you will quickly see that many of the poor people in America have poor minds that create poor habits, but they are not poor. They wear designer clothes, have nice cars, and have the opportunity to attend school for free. The poor people in America spend more than people in poverty in other countries, and that it's not just about how much money you make or save but how you manage your finances. What I am trying to highlight is the need for financial education and awareness among low-income communities, because the money is there; they just don't believe it because of what they see day to day.

WHAT NOW?

The lost art of teaching how to think,
not what to think, needs to be revived.
Born ignorant—not stupid.

We come into this world without any preconceived notions or biases. We are like a blank slate, ready to absorb and learn from our surroundings. However, as we grow older and more influenced by society, we start to develop certain beliefs and perspectives. We are taught to see things from one side, whether it be through education, media, or cultural norms.

The problem with this is that it limits our understanding and prevents us from gaining a more comprehensive view of the world. We become trapped in a narrow mindset, unable to see beyond our own limited perspectives. Ignorance arises when we fail to acknowledge and challenge these preconceptions. To combat ignorance, we need to actively seek new experiences and learn from them. Life itself becomes our greatest teacher. Through interactions with different people, exposure to new cultures, exploration of various ideas, and continuous learning, we can broaden our horizons and overcome the limitations imposed by our learned biases.

Questioning the doctrines and teachings that we have been exposed to is crucial to breaking free from ignorance. It is through critical thinking and open-mindedness that we can challenge the beliefs that have been ingrained within us. We should not accept everything at face value but instead, constantly question, analyze, and re-evaluate what we have been taught.

We must organize, strengthen ourselves and our communities.

- buy collectively as a group
- protect our women and children
- create avenues for more doctors, lawyers, judges, teachers, coaches, police men
- protect and build up one another
- educate our own
- look for every opportunity to start a business, servicing the needs of people

Here are some ideas for how young individuals can uplift their neighborhoods:

1. Volunteer: Encourage them to become active volunteers in local organizations or initiatives. They can support local schools, community centers, or

nonprofit organizations that work towards community development.

2. Mentorship: Encourage them to share their skills
   and knowledge with younger kids by becoming
   mentors or tutors. This can help inspire and empower the next generation.

3. Organize cleanup events: They can take the initiative to organize cleanup campaigns in their neighborhoods to improve its appearance and promote
   cleanliness.

4. Start community gardens: Encourage them to
   transform vacant lots into green spaces where community members can come together, grow their
   own food, and learn about sustainable practices.

5. Advocate for change: Encourage them to join or
   start youth organizations that address social issues and advocate for positive changes within their
   community.

6. Entrepreneurship: Support and mentor young en-
   trepreneurs who are interested in starting their own
   businesses. This can create economic opportunities
   within the community while keeping young people
   engaged and invested in their neighborhood.

By doing these things, we can improve the overall well-being and empowerment of our community. When we organize and come together, we can amplify our voices and push
for positive change. By collectively buying goods and ser-

vices, we can support local businesses and create economic opportunities within our community. It is crucial to protect our women and children, as they are often more vulnerable to various forms of violence and discrimination. By creating avenues for professions such as doctors, lawyers, judges, teachers, coaches, and police officers within our community, we can ensure that our people have access to essential services and representation. Building each other up and providing education for our own community members can lead to a stronger and more self-sufficient community. Lastly, starting businesses that cater to the needs of our people can generate both economic growth and job opportunities within our community.